The past, their pain just slipped away

There was only Jake now, and she ached to feel his body shudder in pleasure against hers.

"Kate, you're as hungry as I am," Jake groaned as her lips pressed tiny urgent kisses against his throat. "The lovers you've had can't have known how to please you." His words chilled her heated flesh, bringing back|all the misery she had endured through this man.

"If you're hungry, Jake, tell Rita!" she managed to say coolly, as she pulled away from him.

"I'd forgotten that was always your favorite game, Kate," he told her savagely, "but you can't always play without getting burned. If I ache for satisfaction tonight, I'll at least know you're aching, too." He grabbed one of the rolled-up sleeping bags and tossed it over to her. "Sweet dreams...."

Books by Penny Jordan

These books may be available at your local bookseller.

For a list of all titles currently available,
send your name and address to:

Harlequin Reader Service
P.O. Box 52040, Phoenix, AZ 85072-2040
Canadian address: P.O. Box 2800, Postal Station A,
5170 Yonge St., Willowdale, Ont. M2N 5T5

PENNY JORDAN

the inward storm

Harlequin Books

TORONTO • NEW YORK • LONDON
AMSTERDAM • PARIS • SYDNEY • HAMBURG
STOCKHOLM • ATHENS • TOKYO • MILAN

Harlequin Presents first edition August 1984
ISBN 0-373-10713-7

Original hardcover edition published in 1984
by Mills & Boon Limited

CHAPTER ONE

As always when she drove down Woolerton's main street Kate felt a warm glow of contentment. Moving to Yorkshire from London had been the best thing she had ever done. She loved the Yorkshire Dales with their ageless grandeur, and she also loved the villages with their clusters of stone-built cottages, their gritty timelessness that said they had withstood for centuries and would continue to do so for many centuries to come. If man allowed them to do so. She grimaced faintly, as she stopped her small car outside the woolshop she owned jointly with her friend and partner Margaret Bowes.

When she had first come to Woolerton she had been looking for escape, and she had not visualised, when she bought the small, out-of-date handicrafts shop, just how successful and stimulating a career she would make of it; a career that now took her regularly to London and New York, where the hand-knitted jumpers she designed and had knitted by her faithful local circle of workers were pounced on avidly by the buyers of top stores. And this latest batch far surpassed anything they had done before, Kate thought enthusiastically as she climbed out of her car, opening the hatchback to remove the garments she had spent the day collecting.

At first when she had approached local farmers' wives, though the medium of the vicar's wife, to ask if they would be interested in knitting up the patterns she designed, they had been sceptical, but once they had discovered how well the jumpers sold, their enthusiasm had kept pace with Kate's own, and now she had a regular circle of knitters, all of whose work she could rely on. Dales wives learned young how to pass the cold dark evenings when their husbands were out with the stock, and this latest batch had been finished well ahead of schedule. Tomorrow she and Margaret could sort and pack the garments ready for despatch.

'Ah, there you are. I was just about to close up,' Margaret smiled in welcome as Kate walked in.

'I stopped off to see Sarah,' Kate explained. Sarah Keddy was one of her favourite knitters, and one of the oldest. There had been Keddys in Ebbdale as long as there had been an Ebbdale, but Sarah Keddy was now alone. Her grandson and his wife, together with their children, had emigrated to New Zealand two years before Kate came to the valley, and although she had many friends Kate knew she suffered from their absence. The hill farm that had been her home for so many years had had to be sold after her husband's death and now she had a cottage at the far end of the village.

She was a 'warm' woman, or so Kate had been told by some of her other knitters, but there was never any evidence of wealth in the tiny but immaculately clean terraced cottage down by the river; rather the opposite. In many ways life in the valley was still hard, but Kate wouldn't change it for luxurious city living. It was here in Woolerton that she had found peace and hope for the future after.... Her mind swerved violently away from the past, as always reluctant to dwell on the events that had brought her to Ebbdale.

Two years had passed since then. Two years in which she had grown new tissue over the old scars. But new tissue didn't totally obliterate the pain; and tranquillity couldn't entirely wipe away her sense of failure at having a broken marriage behind her.

Margaret had helped her so much in those early days. Kate had found Woolerton by accident. Driven mad by a need to get away from London she had driven north, heading for Scotland, but her car had broken down just outside Woolerton, and Meg had then been working in the Woolerton Arms where she had gone to enquire if they had a room for the night.

The one day it was to have taken to get her car back on to the road became three and then four, and by the fifth day Kate had known that she never wanted to leave this quiet valley. Meg, widowed and on the point of being made redundant, had leapt at Kate's suggestion that they buy the craft shop, and although they did quite a brisk trade in local crafts in the summer months and during the winter wool always sold well, it was from the jumpers Kate designed that they made the majority of their profits.

'Matt's picking me up in half an hour,' Meg told her, as she relieved Kate of the pile of jumpers. 'There's a cottage pie in the oven. . . .'

Meg had taken on a new lease of life since she met Matt Wrexley, Kate mused as her friend went upstairs to change for her date with the hill farmer. Widowed like Meg, they had met through his daughter who attended the local Youth Club where Meg helped out three evenings a week. That they would marry Kate did not doubt, although in the Dales such things were not rushed. What would she do when they did? She would have to employ someone in the shop for those days when she was visiting her knitters or away seeing buyers. Time enough to worry about that when it happened, Kate reflected as she locked up the shop and followed Meg upstairs to the small flat they shared above the shop.

As Meg switched on the light, warmth flooded the pale apricot-painted room. Meg had been slightly dubious when Kate explained how she wanted to decorate the flat, but the shop property was Kate's, bought with the mortgage she had raised when they first set up in business, and Meg had been generous in her praise when she saw the finished results.

Rusts, apricots and soft creams dominated the colour scheme, the cane furniture was glossed in the same apricot as the walls, the cushions covered in cream cotton with a rust and apricot design. The floorboards had been stained and a couple of beautifully soft sheepskin rugs were their only covering.

Meg disappeared into her bedroom, while Kate wandered into the kitchen, checking on the cottage pie. When she had lived in London she would have laughed at anything as homely as cottage pie. Orphaned very young, Kate had been brought up by a sophisticated godmother, many times divorced, who spent her life travelling from one glamour spot to another, trailing Kate in her wake as soon as she was old enough to leave school. It had been a hedonistic existence and one which Kate would have said she enjoyed . . . until she met Jake.

At first she had thought he was one of Lyla's latest young men, but even at twenty she had dimly perceived that Jake lacked the malleability Lyla looked for in her handsome escorts. He was too hard, too ungiving to ever be at the beck and call of a woman like Lyla; pretty and vague as a butterfly. And Lyla had been nervous of him. Kate had sensed it that night at dinner. They had been staying in Cannes; they always spent June in Cannes, and she remembered that Lyla had introduced him with that girlish laugh of hers as 'my stepson, darling . . . Jake Harvey.' And Kate had realised that this Jake Harvey must be the son of one of Lyla's many husbands. Lyla's last venture into matrimony had ended just as Kate left school and she had long since forgotten the names of Lyla's various husbands. Her heart had started to thump as Jake Harvey studied her, insolently, she thought as her heartbeat increased, her cheeks flushing as she realised the sexual speculation behind the ice-sharp grey glance.

'Jake, you're embarrassing the child,' Lyla had said sharply, and he had smiled sardonically, releasing her from that hard grey imprisonment. She had wondered about him later that night when Lyla dismissed her, saying that she and Jake had business to discuss. Had his father looked anything like him? If so, no wonder the marriage hadn't lasted long. For all his powerfully male good looks, the lean arrogant body that was so vibrantly masculine that even she had been aware of its potency, there was something about him that chilled and repelled her, a hardness of purpose perhaps, a taunting insistence that where he was concerned there was no other will but his. She would have been well advised to listen to those earlier misgivings, Kate sighed, when Meg emerged from her room, her face faintly flushed. 'How do I look?'

Matt was taking her out to dinner, and Kate assured her that the silk blouse and velvet skirt she was wearing looked very attractive. 'Not mutton dressed as lamb?' she asked anxiously, grinning a little when Kate exploded into laughter and teased, 'Definitely not! Matt would recognise that immediately, as a sheep farmer. Meg, you're forty-five, not ninety,' she added, sobering up a little.

'But that still makes me old enough to be your mother,' Meg reminded her dryly. 'You're the one who should be going out on dates, not me.'

'No, thanks.' Kate had her back to her, pretending to fiddle with the oven.

'Kevin Hargreaves is keen on you, I'm sure,' Meg pressed, mentioning their local doctor. 'He must have telephoned you half a dozen times last week.'

'That was just to arrange about the petition to stop any expansion of the nuclear plant,' Kate told her firmly. 'Oh, why do they want to expand it still more?' she complained, her eyes bitter with hopelessness. 'Don't they realise the potential danger—not just for this valley, for possibly the whole country? Disarmament is the only way, and the politicians have got to be made to realise. . . .'

'Kate, I know how strongly you feel about all this,' Meg told her softly, 'but sometimes strong views can be blinkering. Have you thought how many jobs the plants provide? Without those jobs the valley would be almost bereft of young people. We have to find new forms of power for the future. . . .'

'New ways to maim and destroy,' Kate said bitterly. It was an argument they had had often before. Meg didn't share her views on nuclear disarmament, but Kevin Hargreaves did. Like her, he was keen to form a group of protesters against further expansion of the plant.

An hour later when she had eaten her shepherd's pie and cleared away the dishes Kate sat down, intending to work on some fresh designs for their spring range, but her mind, normally so active, refused to be confined to the work in hand. Instead she found herself thinking about Jake; something she had not allowed herself to do except in brief snatches since their break-up. They should never have married in the first place, and, she suspected, had she been a more sophisticated twenty-one; had she not been living with Lyla, all they would have had would have been a brief affair. Jake had been at first disbelieving and then openly amused when he discovered her innocence. He had told her after they were married that once he did know he couldn't leave her to be destroyed by the style of life Lyla enjoyed.

'Such an intense, emotional little thing,' he had said huskily in that deep voice he used when he was making love to her, the sound shivering across her aroused senses and barely impinging until much later. 'Everything you feel, you feel so deeply. . . .'

She had been a child to Jake; a child who had given herself trustingly to him, and who had married him without a thought of what marriage really entailed, living only for the times when he held her in his arms, turning her body to boneless, liquid fire. But the honeymoon couldn't last for ever. He had a job to do, Jake had reminded her. That job had been at Greenham air-base, using his knowledge to perfect missiles which could destroy hundreds of thousands of innocent people.

She had been such an innocent. Kate shivered, remembering how angry Jake had been when he came home to find her studying the literature the anti-

nuclear faction had put through their door. His anger
had chilled her, as had his insistence that she throw
the stuff away. It was almost as though he wouldn't
allow her to have any views that weren't his; as though
she were a mechanical doll designed purely for his
pleasure and nothing else. And that had been how it
had started. She had revolted against his veto, calling
him a petty dictator and worse. That night he had
made love to her with angry intensity and she had
resisted him; not with her body—that was impossible—
but with her mind. A chasm seemed to have opened
up beneath her feet and with every day that passed it
grew deeper and wider, until she no longer even
wanted to cross it. She became involved with the
Peace Movement, and Jake had been furious. How
well she remembered the row they had had about it. If
she had nothing better to do with her time than waste
it with a bunch of hysterical women then he would
give her something to keep her busy, he had stormed
at her—a child.

And she had screamed back that a child of his was
the last thing she wanted; that she would never give
birth to the child of a man who felt as he did; that she
would never have a child that could be destroyed by
its father's monstrous obsession with destruction. And
so it had gone on, day after day, week after week, until
that final row. It had been just before Christmas, the
annual dance at the base. They had been invited, and
she hadn't wanted to go, but Jake had insisted. So she
had gone, and it had been in a mood of burning
resentment that she had responded to the overtures of
some of the other guests and the base personnel,
letting her views and hatred of what they were doing
spill out into the silence that gradually grew in

intensity until it reached Jake and they were staring at one another down the length of the room, antagonists in a bitter conflict in which there could be no end.

He had taken her home and she had trembled inwardly in fear and anger, but the words he had spoken were not those she had anticipated. He had stood in the door to their bedroom, watching her with cold eyes, and he had said simply, 'This can't go on. I married a child thinking she would mature into womanhood, but all she has done is regress into adolescent puerility. I'm leaving you, Kate. If you ever manage to grow up you can come and find me, but don't expect me to hang around and wait.' He had gone without another word, and she had left the house in the morning, driving north, not wanting to wait until he came back, in case she made a complete fool of herself and begged him to change his mind. She had written to Lyla, who had recommended a lawyer—her own, and who had offered her a home, but she had grown up enough by then to know that Lyla's life style was not hers.

That had been two years ago. The last time she had been in London she had called to see her lawyer to ask what progress he had made with their divorce, but he had told her that Jake was not willing to divorce her.

Her stunned 'But why?' had brought a brief smile to his mouth.

'Many men find it . . . convenient to let their marriages stand in such cases. It affords them splendid protection,' he had added dryly, when she looked puzzled. 'They have their freedom and they also have protection.'

How like Jake, Kate had thought at the time, even now he was still using her. Her eyes filmed over as she felt the familiar tug of memory, and tried not to give in to it, but to concentrate on what she was doing, but the pattern she was working on blurred in front of her, and as clearly as though he was in the room with her she could hear Jake saying softly, 'My little Cat, when I touch you like this you're as boneless and sensual as any feline of the species.'

Her throat dry, Kate started to shiver, passing her tongue over dry lips suddenly tormented by memories she had suppressed ever since they parted. Her skin seemed to burn as she remembered the way Jake had touched her; there had been nothing adolescent about her reaction to him, nor the way his body had taught her to respond to his lovemaking. But that was only a memory now. She had not allowed any man to get close enough to her to make love to her since and she had no intention of doing so. The male instinct to possess and repress was as strong today as it had always been; man wanted woman in his bed subservient to his desires, and she could never forget that Jake had dismissed her views and thoughts as carelessly as though they were those of a two-year-old. He had frightened her the first time she had seen him, that aura of power and masculinity he possessed overwhelming her, but in the sexual haze of wanting him she had forgotten to be afraid, and that had been her downfall.

What on earth was she doing allowing her thoughts to meander down such dead ends, Kate thought tiredly, thrusting her work aside and running slim fingers through the chestnut mass of curls that reached down to her shoulders. Lyla had wanted her to have her hair cut that summer she met Jake, and that had been the first time she had realised that he wanted her, the day he had looked at her and said sharply, 'No, leave her hair as it is, Lyla,' to her stepmother, adding under his breath, 'One day some man's going to thank you for it when he sees it fanned out across his pillow . . .' and she had known that Jake wasn't thinking in terms of 'some man' but himself. How that knowledge had excited her! She bit her lip, trying not to remember, irritated to discover that it was only nine o'clock. Far too early to go to bed. The ringing of the telephone was a welcome relief.

'Kate?' She recognised Kevin Hargreaves' voice instantly and responded to it warmly. 'I thought you might like to know that they've appointed a new Head of Operations at the station. I found out about it today.' Kevin was one of the doctors on stand-by for the plant, and he went on to explain that although he had no other details about the new appointee he was hoping to persuade him to adopt several new safety measures.

'Oh, safety measures!' Kate exploded. 'They're all very well in their way, but what we should be campaigning for is to get the plant closed down completely.'

Kevin's chuckle reached her from the other end of the wire. 'That's impossible, I'm afraid, Kate. Nuclear power is here to stay, and that's a fact of life. If we can just get them to adopt a more aware attitude to the possibilities I'd be well pleased. As soon as I find out who the new Director is I'm going to invite him round for dinner. I was hoping you might cook it for me and play hostess,' he added, coaxingly. 'Mrs Mac is all very well in her way, but she isn't a patch on you. It will give you an opportunity to put forward your views as well,' he added. When Kate agreed he thanked her and rang off, explaining that it was his evening on call and that he couldn't stay too long on the phone in case any emergency calls came through. At least Kevin wasn't like Jake, Kate thought when she had replaced the receiver. He accepted that she had her own views and listened to them, but pleasant though he was Kevin did nothing for her sexually; he was a pleasant, attractive man in his mid-thirties, and she liked him as a friend, but there was none of the electricity Jake had generated. Jake had been thirty when she first met him and even then there had been a forcefulness about him, a raw maleness that alarmed even when it aroused, and she had been young and silly enough to be excited by the fear his potential to dominate and master had aroused inside her. It was only later that she had learned to despise that need to dominate and to despise herself for ever wanting it.

It was quite late when Meg returned. Kate was already in bed, but she heard her come in, and she was shocked to discover that she was wondering if Meg, like her, ever missed the warm male presence in her bed at night.

'So when's the wedding to be?' They were in the shop sorting out the jumpers Kate had collected the previous day, the solitaire diamond on Meg's left hand winking brightly as her fingers moved deftly through the pile.

'Oh, not until next summer. In the lull between lambing and shearing,' Meg twinkled, flushing a little as she added half shyly, 'I still can't believe I've been so lucky. David and I married young and I was so happy with him. I thought I'd never get over his death, and I certainly never dreamed I'd find the kind of happiness with anyone else that I've found with Matt.'

'I'll have to start looking for someone to work in the shop after Christmas,' Kate told her. 'Any ideas?'

'What about Lucy?'

Lucy was Matt's daughter, a pleasant plump girl of seventeen. 'She wants to find a job, and Matt and I both think she's far too young to leave the valley yet. She was thinking of going for secretarial work and finding herself a job at the plant, but she's a marvellous knitter, and rather on the quiet side.' Meg glanced thoughtfully at Kate. 'You know, Kate, the girls at the youth club would enjoy a few lessons from you on the design aspects of knitting. You stay in far too much, and this bee you've got in your bonnet about the station. Most of the people round here welcome it. There's the jobs, for one thing. . . .'

'They welcome it because they have no other choice,' Kate said fiercely, 'Do you think they would honestly welcome it if they knew that it could maim and kill their children; that the mere existence of places like Greenham means that Russian missiles are constantly directed towards this country. . . .'

'Ebbdale doesn't have a missile base,' Meg told her quietly, 'It has a nuclear power station, and missiles give protection as well as making us a target.'

'With multilateral disarmament missiles wouldn't be needed,' Kate argued, but Meg merely sighed.

'Oh, my dear,' she said softly, 'human beings aren't like that. Can't you see? You only have to look at children, any group of children, to see the tendencies that are inside all of us to dominate and manoeuvre. Wonderful though it would be if human beings could live in peace with one another, first we all have to be capable of giving and receiving absolute trust, of making ourselves acutely vulnerable, a fundamental something which the majority of the human race is incapable of doing, the flaw that makes us human.'

Even though part of Kate knew that Meg was right, stubbornly she refused to admit it. These arguments were old and much used ones, but that did not make them right. How vividly she remembered how she had felt when Jake talked about them having a child. A child who would be forced to live and grow under the threat of the nuclear holocaust his own father had helped to build against him. And if that threat was not averted, and there was war, how many generations into the future would be maimed and diseased because of it? It didn't bear thinking about.

A phone call from one of their knitters on one of the more remote hill farms had Kate setting out in her small car immediately after lunch to collect the jumpers she had ready. It took her about an hour to reach the farm, and she was warmly greeted by Beth Carr as she got out of the car and walked across the cobbled yard.

A heavenly scent of baking bread greeted her when she followed Beth into the kitchen. Cookery was another skill Kate had developed since coming to the Dales. When she lived with Jake they had often eaten out, or she had bought convenience foods. 'Umm, one of the best smells on earth,' Kate commented as Beth indicated one of the chairs beside the fire.

'I finished the last jumper last night,' Beth told her, 'and I'm afraid I won't be able to do any more for a while.'

'Oh, Beth!' Kate was surprised when Beth turned towards her, her plump face wreathed in smiles.

'It's happened at last,' she told her proudly. 'I'm having a baby. After all these years, Pete and I had stopped hoping, but Dr Hargreaves has confirmed it, and from now on all my knitting will be white and small.'

'Beth, I'm so pleased for you.' Kate knew how unhappy Beth had been at her inability to conceive, and was genuinely pleased for her, even though it meant losing one of her best workers.

'I think I've found you another knitter, though,' Beth told her cheerfully. 'Pete's cousin—she lives out Highmoor way. I was getting that worried about telling you I couldn't do any more, Pete went down and asked her. Said he wasn't having me fretting myself into flinders. Not now.' Her hand rested fondly against her stomach and Kate was attacked by the most acute sense of pain and deprivation. What on earth was the matter with her? 'We were happy enough before, I suppose,' Beth said softly, 'but there's nothing like knowing you're carrying your man's child inside you. Sort of makes you feel complete, somehow. And as for Pete . . .' she gave a warm laugh, 'well, he's like a dog with two tails and no mistake. Anyone would think no man had ever had a child before, but then it takes some of them that way, I suppose, and we've waited that long.'

For some reason Kate was glad to escape from the warmth of the farm kitchen, glad of the cold biting wind from the east that burned into her still vulnerable skin and brought the sting of tears to her eyes. What on earth was the matter with her? she asked herself bitterly as she wrenched the car round and headed back towards the road. Just for a moment then in the kitchen she had wished . . . no, *longed*, to be able to share Beth's happiness, to feel Jake's child inside her, with a feeling just as intense as that she had experienced when she had denied him. She could barely understand her own emotions. It was as though a stranger had suddenly appeared inside her skin, masquerading as her. She hadn't wanted Jake's child because she couldn't bear to think of bringing a child into the world in which they lived—besides, there had been Jake's arrogant assumption that he could impose his will on hers; that he could simply announce that they would have a child and that was it! He hadn't so much as consulted her. Treating her like a child, refusing to listen to her views . . . calling her an idealistic adolescent.

'Umm, you missed a treat,' Meg told her when she got back. 'Rita's just left. She was full of the man who's taken over from Henry Cousins at the station. You should have seen her, she was practically drooling over him! According to her he's superman and Apollo all rolled into one, and very, very macho with it.'

'They should make a good pair, then,' Kate said snappily. She didn't care very much for Rita Sutcliffe, the daughter of Woolerton's wealthiest man. She was reed-slim, blonde, with the instincts of a tigress defending her kill when it came to men, and Kate and Rita had never got on together. Rita had openly taunted Kate for her views about the station. As far as Rita was concerned, it was a new source of men, and since Rita much preferred being a large fish in the very small pool of Ebbdale to living as a very small fish indeed in London, new men were always of interest to her. She was a sensual egotist who made no secret of her enjoyment of the same sort of hedonistic life so much enjoyed by Lyla, and Kate knew that secretly Rita despised her just as much as she disliked the other woman.

'I'm sure they will if Rita has anything to do with it. You didn't tell me that Kevin is planning to throw a "welcome to Woolerton" dinner party for him? Rita was most put out to learn that Kevin has asked you to act as his hostess for it.'

'Primarily because he wants me to do the cooking,' Kate assured her dryly.

'Umm. Our dear Rita might be a Cordon Bleu between the sheets, but in the kitchen she's a real no-hoper!' They both laughed. 'By the way,' Meg added, 'Rita bought one of the new sweaters. You might not like her,' she added to Kate, 'but she's good for business. We got at least half a dozen sales from the last one she bought. Her father has influential friends all over the Dales, and Rita gets around.'

'In every sense of the expression,' Kate agreed sardonically. She would have to ring Kevin to find out exactly what arrangements he was making for this dinner party. She grimaced. Rita couldn't have been too pleased to discover that Kevin had asked her to be his hostess. Until her arrival Rita had looked upon Kevin as very much a member of her court, and she hadn't appreciated his defection. Not that she needed to worry. Kevin did nothing for her except as a friend. Jake had called her a delightful little sensualist, but that part of her nature seemed to have died with her love for him, and certainly she doubted that any man would see anything sensual about her now, she reflected, studying her reflection subjectively in the mirror which hung in the shop. Small, barely five foot four, her jeans clinging to hips that were almost

boyishly slim, accentuating the fullness of breasts Kate
had always privately thought too full. Her face, free of
make-up, was almost triangular in shape, her eyes
large and slightly almond-shaped, a dark, dense
sapphire colour, oddly exotic in the creamy pallor of
her skin. With her chestnut hair tumbling down round
her shoulders she looked closer to eighteen than the
twenty-four she would be next month, and Lyla would
have a fit if she could see the way she was dressed. Her
aunt had always insisted on her wearing sophisticated
and expensive clothes. That was one thing she could
say about Lyla, she had never stinted when it came to
money. Why, the wedding dress she had bought
her. . . .

Kate heaved a sigh. She was dwelling far too much
on the past. It wasn't good for her, especially when
she had vowed to put it all behind her. But Jake had
been furious about that dress she couldn't help
remembering, saying it was far too sophisticated for
her, and demanding to know why pale peach when she
had every right to wear white? She could remember
how worried she had been, worried about offending
Lyla and worried because Jake was so annoyed. She
had told him she was still a virgin the day he proposed
to her, or rather he had proposed after she had told
him. And that in itself ought to have been a warning,
only she had been too bemused to see it. According to
his views he had probably been doing the honourable
thing, marrying her instead of merely making love to
her, but in the long run it would have been kinder
simply to have taken her innocence, initiated her into
womanhood and then gone . . . kinder and far less
painful than a marriage built on desire on one
partner's side and infatuation on the other. Even while

adoring him she had resented him, Kate reflected, savouring the knowledge, knowing she had never realised it before. She had resented him for inhabiting a world which was still barred to her, for being adult and experienced, for controlling her as though she were a wooden puppet on a string, for eliciting responses from her body she hadn't known they could feel ... the list was endless.

'Kate, phone,' Meg called. 'It's Kevin. He wants to talk to you.'

'It's all fixed, Kate,' Kevin told her. 'Next Wednesday, if that's okay with you. I spoke to Harvey myself. He seems quite a pleasant sort, but extremely decisive ... Kate? Are you still there?'

Part of her was, Kate thought numbly, the rest was still trying to come to terms with what Kevin had just said. 'Did he ... do you know his first name?' she croaked.

'His first name?' Kevin sounded puzzled. 'Oh yes, let me see. It's Jay ... or. ...'

'Jake,' Kate supplemented, having known the answer long before Kevin gave it. It was too much of a coincidence to expect another man in Jake's field to share his surname.

'Yes, that's right ... heard of him, have you?' Kevin chuckled. 'I've warned him about you. Our anti-nuclear firebrand!' Her palm was moist where it came into contact with the phone. 'By name?' she managed through a dry aching throat, 'or merely by reputation?'

'Oh, by name,' Kevin told her. 'He wanted to know who his fellow guests were to be.'

'Yes, he would, and that meant that she could hardly back out now. How he would gloat if she did, knowing that she had preferred flight to fight. Dear

God, Jake here! How could it have happened? How could the fates have chosen with such fine irony, destroying the fragile shell she had built for herself? Was Jake planning to turn Ebbdale into a missile storehouse? Her lip curled bitterly. This time she wouldn't let him toss aside her arguments and destroy all her objections. This time she would show him. . . . And she would start by hostessing Kevin's dinner. She would show Jake that he couldn't exert any power over her any longer. She was free and she was adult. Ex-husbands and wives met on countless of thousands of occasions these days; there was nothing of any note in it.

It was only as she replaced the receiver that the final irony struck her. Rita's fabulous new man was *her* husband. So why did she feel more like howling than laughing? And Jake, what was he feeling right now? Nothing, she assured herself tartly, she knew enough to know that in fact he was probably deriving sadistic amusement from the potential of the situation. He must have known she was up here. Lyla would have told him, just as she had kept her informed of his movements. Poor Lyla, for all the fact that she had been married so often herself she had never ceased to try and get them back together, but she had ignored all her well-meaning hints, and presumably Jake had done the same. The last she had heard about him was that he was working in the States, and she had half expected that he would make his life out there. Perhaps he had found the powerful pressure of the American lobbying groups too much for him, she thought grimly, wondering as she did so if she wasn't being a little too sanguine. Nothing would be too much for Jake; he was tough and he was enduring, and he would relish the conflict.

Just for a moment she contemplated flight, but the moment was quickly gone. She had built a life here, she would still be here when Jake had gone on to the next prestige appointment. She would not be panicked into flight. Woolerton was now her home, she was accepted, she had friends; tolerant, kind friends who even when they didn't share her views permitted her to express them, and listened politely, friends who didn't dismiss her as a fractious child, and she wasn't giving them up because of Jake!

CHAPTER TWO

KATE shopped for Kevin's dinner party with special care, telling herself that it was quite natural that she should want to impress, but refusing to admit that it was Jake the man her efforts were aimed at and not Jake Harvey, Director of the Nuclear Power Station.

Two other couples had been invited, and Rita, and Kate wasn't entirely surprised when the other girl called into the shop and dropped casually into the conversation the fact that Jake was collecting her.

'I hope you've got something decent to wear, darling,' she murmured when she left. 'I've told Kevin to make it formal. We don't get enough opportunities to dress up in these benighted parts. He tells me he's taking you to the Hunt Ball?' She smiled and inspected her nails, almost purring with pleasure as she drawled, 'Jake's taking me. Daddy always makes up a party and of course we'll be going with them. He'll be spending the night with us of course.'

For 'us' read 'me', Kate thought cynically when Rita had gone. Really, it was almost farcical; there was Rita telling her that she intended spending the night with Jake, not realising that Jake was her husband. Not that she cared who he spent his nights with. She had once, though. Dear God, the pangs of jealousy she had endured, too insecure and vulnerable to deceive herself that Jake cared for her alone, every beautiful woman who glanced at him was a potential rival, and many had glanced at him, and more.

Kevin's father had been Woolerton's doctor before him and his house, which was simply referred to as 'the doctor's house', was a four-square Victorian building just off the High Street, a brick wall enclosing the lawned gardens. The house was still furnished as it had been during Kevin's grandparents' time and he had given Kate carte blanche as far as the dinner party was concerned. It wasn't the first time she had cooked for him, and Mrs MacDonald, who came in to do his cleaning, promised to wash and iron the damask tablecloth Kate unearthed and to help polish the Victorian silver.

'Got some lovely things, the doctor has,' she sighed as she and Kate worked together in the old-fashioned kitchen. 'Wasted on a man, they are.' A speculative glance followed the words, but Kate didn't rise to the bait, and with another sigh, this time one of disappointment, Mrs MacDonald returned to her polishing.

Rather appropriate for a sheep-rearing area, Kate had decided to serve rack of lamb with the accompaniment of a special sauce she had discovered in one of Kevin's grandmother's cookery books. The first course was to be melon sorbet, made with a puree of the fruit of the melon and cream which was then frozen to the texture of ice cream. She had also decided to serve a fish course and had opted for fresh salmon. To follow the rack of lamb there would be chocolate soufflé which she knew Kevin loved and some delicate meringue swans which looked attractive but which were relatively simple to make. A cheese board and a selection of fresh fruit would take care of those guests who eschewed a sweet finale to their meal.

Kevin's other guests were the Master of the local Hunt and his wife, who were also the largest local landowners; a pleasant couple whom Kate had met on several occasions and whose company she enjoyed, and a friend of Kevin's from York, a barrister who had been at Cambridge with him, and whom Kate had met only once previously but also liked. His wife was an interior designer and they had turned their backs on London to return to Yorkshire. Like Kate, Lisa Flemming was a keen anti-nuker, to use the American term. All of them knew that she had been married and was separated, but none of them, not even Meg, knew who her husband was. Kate had wondered if she ought to tell Kevin, but although they were good friends there was no romantic involvement between them, and the knowledge that she and Jake were man and wife was embarrassing enough without extending that embarrassment to anyone else. After all, Jake was hardly likely to bring it up; not if he was escorting Rita, who presumably believed him to be 'free' and 'available'.

Because she was preparing the meal, Kate decided it would be as well to change into her evening clothes at Kevin's. The large Victorian house had any number of spare bedrooms, and when she arrived with her case on Wednesday morning, Mrs MacDonald expressed benevolent approval. 'You can use the room next to the doctor's. It used to be his parents', and it's got its own bathroom. Makes no sense rushing back to that shop to get changed and then risking getting a chill.'

It was a particularly cold day, autumn already giving way to winter several weeks too early. Most of the trees were denuded of their leaves, but Kate had grown used to the brief Northern springs and summers, both all the more poignantly lovely because of their brevity. As she had promised, Mrs MacDonald had paid special attention to the drawing room and dining room. Kevin rarely used them except when he was entertaining, and Kate was glad she had had the foresight to suggest that he turned their radiators on at the beginning of the week. Both rooms had working fires, and both were laid ready to be lit. The flowers she had ordered from the nearby town had also arrived, russets and bronzes to tone with the gold and green of the traditional dinner service she and Mrs MacDonald had unearthed. It was lunchtime before they had finished, the polished mahogany table gleaming under its weight of silver and crystal, Kate's floral arrangement the single note of colour on the damask cloth.

'Looks a rare fine sight, it does,' Mrs MacDonald approved, when she came in with a silver salver of sherry glasses. 'He's a lucky man, is the doctor, having you to do all this for him. There's many as wouldn't have bothered for all that they think themselves the bee's knees,' she added disparagingly, and Kate hid a small grin. She was well aware of the emnity which existed between Rita and Kevin's cleaner. Rita was a great believer in people keeping to their place, which she invariably considered to be beneath hers, and Mrs MacDonald was not a lady who took lightly to being condescended to.

At seven o'clock Kate pulled off her apron with a tiny relieved sigh and went upstairs to luxuriate in the relaxing warmth of her bath. Kevin had just returned, later than expected, and he too was changing. Some impulse she wasn't anxious to examine too carefully had prompted Kate into being generous with the perfume she had poured into her bath. A new one for her, 'Opium', which Lyla had sent her for Christmas, in a lavish coffrette which included body lotion, perfume and talc. As she stepped into the bedroom wrapped in her towelling robe her feet left damp imprints on the carpet, and as she glanced at her watch she was dismayed to see how long she had lingered in the bathroom.

'Kate, are you decent? I can't fix this damned bow tie,' she heard Kevin mutter impatiently outside her door. 'Can't think why Rita insisted on all this formal gear. . . .'

'I expect she's got a new dress she wants to show off,' Kate told him lightly as she opened her door, her mouth creasing in a humorous smile as she surveyed Kevin's harassed features. His mousy hair stood on end and his dinner suit, although well fitting made him look ill at ease. Kevin looked best in the ancient tweed jacket and casual trousers he wore for doing his rounds.

'Come and stand over here under the light,' Kate instructed him, following him as he walked towards the head of the stairs. 'Now I can see what I'm doing.' Because she was not particularly tall, it was still necessary for Kate to stand on tiptoe to reach upwards to fiddle with the intricate fastening of Kevin's bow tie. She was just on the point of succeeding when they heard the doorbell.

'Damn,' Kevin swore, and swivelled his head automatically, undoing all Kate's careful handiwork. 'It's only quarter to eight! Who the devil. . . .'

Mrs MacDonald, who had expressed a formidable determination to stay and as she put it 'help with the siding away', bustled into the hall and called out to

Kate, 'Don't worry, I'll get it.' She opened the door, and Kate's heart sank as she heard Rita's familiar shrill voice.

'Oh no, I'm sure you're wrong,' she was saying. 'I know Kate told me seven-thirty. . . .' She paused on the threshold, peering round with extravagant bewilderment. Damn her, Kate thought grimly. She knew Rita of old, and she had no doubts at all that her early arrival was designed to cause an upset, but she had succeeded way, way, beyond her wildest dreams, Kate acknowledged dazedly as she looked down into the hall and her eyes meshed with the icy grey ones of the man who had followed Rita inside. Had he always been so tall? Six foot two, she remembered, and the fact that she was looking down at him ought to have diminished him, but it didn't. He hadn't changed at all, unless it was to look harder, more determined than ever, and the cold scrutiny in his eyes relayed its own brutal message as he studied the untidy knot of hair on top of her head, down along the curves of her body disguised by the robe she was wearing . . . down . . . down until Kate felt her toes curling into the carpet beneath the protection-stripping acidity of that scrutiny.

'Kate darling, what on earth are you doing?' If anyone could lace arch suggestiveness with coy innocence it was Rita, Kate thought, gritting her teeth.

'Fixing Kevin's bow tie,' she replied coolly, 'but now that you're here perhaps you would like to do it for me, while I get ready.'

'Oh, but of course, darling,' Rita all but purred. 'Poor you . . . did something go wrong, or . . .' Her glance slid sideways from Kate's set face to Kevin's unaware one . . . 'or did we arrive at a bad time?'

'You're early,' Kevin told her. 'You weren't supposed to be here until eight, and I got back late.'

'But, darling, you're ready,' Rita pointed out slyly. 'Kate's been here all day, and she isn't. Having problems, Kate?'

'Not really.' She forced herself to smile calmly. 'Drinks are ready in the drawing room, Kevin. I shan't be long. . . .' She paused by the door to her room.

'Staying the night, are you?' Rita enquired. 'Oh, don't be shy with me, darling,' she added sweetly, 'we're all adults here, although I can well understand why Kevin put you in a separate room. Mrs Mac, Kevin's cleaner, is a regular pillar of the Church,' she explained to Jake, adding, 'Oh, Jake, poor darling—I haven't introduced you yet, have I? This is Kevin, your host, and. . . .'

'Let's let poor Kate get dressed before anyone else arrives,' Kevin suggested, interrupting Rita hastily. 'Sorry about this, Harvey,' Kate heard him apologising to Jake as she closed her bedroom door. 'It's all Rita's fault, if she hadn't insisted on this damned formal dress. . . .'

She couldn't stay here cowering away all night, Kate told herself shakily, hardly able to bear to face her reflection in the mirror. She looked like a child who had been beaten. Defeat lay starkly at the back of her eyes, her skin as pale as skimmed milk. She stared at the dress hanging on the back of the door. She had bought it on a mad impulse in London. Matt black silk, it was American, Calvin Klein, with long tight sleeves and a neckline that dipped almost to the waist at the front, where the silk was caught up in a soft knot, the skirt of the dress caught up in the same way, so that if revealed the slender length of her thighs when she moved. It clung so tightly to her skin that all she could wear beneath it was a pair of fine silk panties. The choker of pearls Lyla had given her as a wedding present did little to make the dress appear more modest, but in reality it revealed far less of her body than Rita's rustling boned-bodiced taffeta. But it was the way it hinted at what wasn't revealed that made it a dress designed by a man for a woman with his own sex in mind, Kate reflected as she brushed her hair and let it settle round her shoulders in a heavy cloud, knowing there wasn't time to do anything else with it. Black high-heeled satin sandals, and the careful application of enough make-up to give her a gloss of colour, completed her preparations, tiny diamond ear studs winking in her ears when she moved and the chestnut curls drifted languorously against her shoulders.

Instead of joining the others in the drawing room she went straight to the kitchen to check on the meal. The vegetables were all prepared ready for cooking when everyone had arrived. Heaving a faint sigh of relief that everything was under control, Kate walked unsteadily into the hall, smoothing slightly damp palms against her hips as she took a deep breath and walked into the drawing room. Conversation stopped. Out of the corner of her eye Kate was aware of Rita regarding her with barely concealed chagrin, Jake at her side, his enigmatical grey glance slicing towards her, warning her that he was not deceived; that he knew she was still the vulnerable child she had always been, despite the trappings of womanhood she was now able to assume.

'Kate . . . Kate, you look magnificent,' Kevin muttered, plainly stunned by her appearance.

'My dear, you did go overboard, didn't you?' Rita said nastily. 'Did you go down to London especially to buy it? You should be honoured, Jake,' she told her companion. 'Kate's normal attire is jeans and an ancient woolly jumper. Kate runs our local craft shop.' She made it sound as though she had straws stuck in her hair, Kate thought irefully. 'She's also a fantastic cook, unlike poor little me!' Rita batted her eyelashes winsomely.

'I bought the dress in London, the last time I went to New York,' Kate interposed coolly. 'Another sherry, Rita? You prefer sweet, don't you?' Heavens, what was getting into her? Kate wondered. She was being nearly as bitchy as Rita. Fortunately the doorbell rang before the situation could deteriorate any further, and as luck would have it Lisa and Richard had arrived at exactly the same time as the Crabtrees.

'Kate, this melon is delicious,' Mary Crabtree enthused when they were halfway through the first course. 'I've never tasted anything like it. By the way, I've made Alan promise to buy me one of your lovely jumpers for Christmas, and I mean to make sure he does,' she added, smiling at her husband. 'Kate designs the most beautiful jumpers,' she told Jake who was seated on her right. 'She sells them in London and New York and has a regular circle of knitters working for her in Ebbdale.'

'She's also absolutely anti your power station, darling,' Rita cut in bitchily. 'I swear she'd have us all dancing around it like those Greenham Common women if she could, wouldn't you, Kate?'

'It's no secret that I disapprove of missiles being based in this country,' Kate agreed smoothly, her eyes meeting Jake's down the length of the table. 'I'm a firm believer in multilateral disarmament, and I'm sorry if you don't approve of that, Mr Harvey.'

'Are you?' Jake challenged softly. Everyone's attention seemed to be riveted on her, Kate realised, and she could sense that Rita was furious at this turn of events. Kate knew quite well that the only reason Rita had mentioned her anti-nuclear stance was to draw it to Jake's attention, not to make Kate the centre of everyone else's.

'Well, I for one admire and agree with Kate,' Lisa was saying. 'Oh, I know you don't agree with me, Richard,' she silenced her husband, 'but the thought of what could happen if a reactor went wrong gives me the shivers, and I can't believe that adequate precautions are taken with the transport of nuclear waste. You only have to read the papers. . . .'

'Yes,' Kevin broke in eagerly, 'that's one aspect of nuclear power that worries me, and it's one I wanted to bring up with you, Jake. During your predecessor's time we campaigned hard to tighten up the safety standards, but Henry was a bit of a diehard. . . . Please don't think we've dragged you here tonight to bombard you with arguments and persuasion but if you could spare the time to talk with me about the safety standards. . . .'

'I am always interested in discussions that could lead to an improvement in that quarter,' Jake surprised Kate by saying smoothly. 'In fact at the station I've been working on in the States, we found there was a marked decrease in antipathy towards nuclear power once we invited the local people in to see how it works. We ran several tours, gave talks, asked them for their views and thoughts, and set up a working committee comprised of some of our staff and the locals ... and you mustn't lose sight of the fact that these stations often bring work to areas of low unemployment. . . .'

'Work, ill health and the potential for death,' Kate interrupted bitterly. He was mesmerising them with his voice, with his reasoned arguments and calm approach, but she wasn't deceived, not for a moment.

'That's a typically female and if you'll forgive me, rather hysterical reaction,' Jake countered coolly. 'Coal mining, engineering, and many other forms of employment are hazardous, but I've yet to see a bunch of hysterical women gathered round a pithead screeching for it to be closed.'

'It isn't just the manner of the work,' Kate protested. 'It's everything that goes with it!'

'If you mean missiles, that isn't the purpose of Ebbdale's station. It's a nuclear power station only. Missiles are a separate entity, but again I can't agree with you. They are a deterrent, whichever way you look at it. In a world of perfect human beings we wouldn't need them, I'd be the first to agree, but unfortunately when Adam bit into that apple, he absorbed more than the mere knowledge of sex; mankind is its own worst enemy. For centuries we've systematically destroyed our planet and our environment. . . .'

'And now you're prepared to go one step further and destroy it completely!'

'Not personally,' Jake assured her grimly. His mouth had tightened and she recognised the icy sparks glittering from the cold grey eyes. He *had* changed, she thought, watching him. There were the faint beginnings of grey in the matt darkness of his hair,

hair she had loved to ruffle beneath her fingers, to stroke as he made love to her. 'Try looking at the other side of the coin,' he advised her harshly. 'Nuclear power could free this planet from starvation and poverty, third world nations. . . .'

'Can't wait to build missiles with it,' Kate interrupted him huskily, 'people are expendable, power is not!'

'Oh, Kate, for goodness' sake,' Rita interrupted pouting a smile at Jake, 'poor Jake came here for a meal, not to be harangued. Honestly, darling, you'd better watch it, you're turning into a fanatic. Kate's divorced, you know,' she confided to Jake, making Kate feel sick inside as she forced herself to look into his implacable face. 'Poor darling, she does tend to get dreadfully intense at times.'

Kate couldn't bear to look at Jake. She excused herself stiltedly and rushed into the kitchen, half blinded by the tears of fury she couldn't suppress. Lisa was behind her, her pretty face pink with sympathy and anger as she closed the kitchen door. 'What a first-rate bitch Rita is,' she announced. 'Personally I'm sure she only did it because she could see how interested Jake was in what you were saying. She's jealous that she might lose him to you.'

'There isn't any danger of that,' Kate assured her, breathing deeply as she tried to regain control.

'Oh, I shouldn't be so sure,' Lisa argued, helping her to load the heated trolley with the main course. 'I saw the way he was looking at you, like a very hungry cat faced with a particularly delectable mouse, and Rita saw it too.'

'Well, she needn't worry,' Kate said hardily, 'He isn't my type. I prefer men whose compassion isn't in inverse proportion to their massively inflated male ego!' She heard Lisa's indrawn breath, and turned quickly, colour flooding her pale face as she saw Jake standing in the door frame, the look in his eyes telling her that he had overheard every rash word.

'Ah, Rita was wrong, I see. She seemed to think you had made a bolt for the kitchen to indulge in a fit of feminine tears. As I seemed to have been responsible for causing them I thought it my duty to come and ensure that you weren't crying saltily into our dinner.'

Kate could tell that Lisa was surprised. She was watching them round-eyed with awe, and Kate supposed that it did seem a highly charged exchange for two people who were only supposed to have met for the first time a couple of hours ago. She wasn't to know that tears had often been her refuge from the acid lash of Jake's tongue, during their marriage. She hadn't cried since he left her, and she certainly wasn't going to start now.

'On the contrary, you'll find your dinner is completely salt-free,' she told him coolly, 'it's far better for one's health.'

'Gracious,' Lisa goggled later when she was helping Kate to remove the main course and bring in the dessert and the cheese, 'he must have heard every word we said! I can't think what would have happened if the two of you had been alone.'

'He'd have strangled me probably,' Kate admitted with a commendable show of uninterest.

'Either that or kissed you breathless,' Lisa agreed. 'And to think he's being wasted on Rita! He makes *me* feel weak at the knees!' She saw Kate's hand shake faintly and pounced. 'Ah, I knew you weren't as indifferent to him as you seemed. If you want my opinion,' she added slyly, 'all that verbal sparring can have only one real conclusion.'

'Yes,' Kate agreed, hiding a small smile as she saw the speculation in Lisa's eyes. 'One of us is going to run out of words—but I promise you it won't be me.'

'Fantastic meal, Kate,' Alan praised when they had all finished. 'Kevin is bringing you to the Hunt Ball, isn't he?'

'Umm, I asked her last week,' Kevin confirmed, 'births and accidents permitting.' There was general laughter, and Lisa explained to Jake that there hadn't been a single year when Kevin had managed to stay the entire length of a Hunt Ball, without a call.

'Do you hunt?' Alan asked him.

'I haven't done, but I do ride.'

'Well, you'll have to join us one Saturday.'

'Don't forget next Saturday we've got a meeting of the Dale Rescue Group,' Kevin reminded him. 'Kate, would you take the minutes for us again this time?'

'I always know winter's on the way when the Rescue Group starts meeting again,' Mary sighed. 'Last year they must have had at least two dozen call-outs over the winter period, mostly from hikers and walkers who simply ask for trouble.'

'Yes, and we're one down this year,' Kevin pointed out. 'Sid Rowanthorpe has dropped out. He's coming up for retirement, and he just doesn't feel he can go on with it, so we'll have to look round for someone else.'

'What's involved exactly?' Jake asked, and when Kevin briefly explained that they needed an extra team member skilled in climbing and mountaincraft, to act as a stretcher bearer for the more severe accidents, he promptly informed them that he had some experience. 'I'm not suggesting I'm up to your standards, it's something I was keen on in my teens, and I've spent several holidays in the Alps and the Rockies.'

'You sound like manna from Heaven,' Kevin said fervently. 'Why don't you come with us on some of our practice climbs? We can see how we all work together as a team.'

Surely she didn't resent the way Jake was fitting into her circle of friends, Kate thought incredulously a couple of hours later when Alan and Mary made a move to leave. She wasn't as childish as that? No, she was still suffering from the strain of seeing him after so long. She had been prepared for it, but still it had been an ordeal, something she had had to steel herself for, and now she was feeling the strain.

'Of course, you won't be leaving, will you, Kate?' Rita said sweetly as she stood up. 'It was so funny when we arrived,' she said to the room at large. 'There was Kate still in her bathrobe, trying to fix Kevin's bow tie. . . .'

'I'm not staying, Rita,' Kate said evenly. 'Kevin was kind enough to let me use his parents' room to get changed in before dinner, so that I didn't need to go home.'

'Honestly, sweetie, it doesn't matter,' Rita assured her mock-sweetly. 'We're all adults, after all . . . I mean, it's not as though you're still sweet seventeen. . . .'

'Rita, that's enough,' Kevin expostulated, suddenly coming to Kate's rescue. 'What you're suggesting is offensive to Kate, and to me. There's no need for either of us to indulge in a hole-and-corner affair, and to suggest that we are is an insult to both of us.'

Rita looked put out, but still pulled a face and murmured, 'Oh, darling, such a fuss about nothing!'

Kate was standing with her back to Jake, and the hair on the back of her neck prickled atavistically as she heard him murmur so quietly that only she could hear, 'But you're not, are you, Kate ... free, that is? Are you lovers, Kate?' she heard him ask.

She whirled round, not caring if anyone saw her, or what interpretation they might put on her behaviour. 'It's none of your damned business,' she ground out through compressed lips.

'Oh, but it is,' Jake assured her smoothly. 'You're still my wife, remember? But you give yourself away, my little Cat,' he added smoothly, 'scratching instead of purring. Whatever our good doctor does give you, it isn't satisfaction.'

'Jake darling, are you ready?' Jake was holding her hand and he raised it to his lips as an old-world gesture of courtliness that deceived everyone but Kate, pressing his lips lightly against her vulnerable palm, leaving her so intensely aware of their roughly warm imprint on her skin that she had to fight not to admit the memories that brief touch brought surging to life.

CHAPTER THREE

'HEAVENS, I'd better rush, Matt will be here in half an hour. What are your plans for the weekend, Kate?' As she spoke Meg put down the cloth she had been using to dry their breakfst dishes and rushed distractedly towards the door.

Sunday mornings were always a panic because invariably they slept later, and Kate obligingly moved to one side to let Meg through the door. 'Kevin and I are going fell-walking. He's been promising to take me for weeks. We did quite a bit of walking during the spring and summer, but the terrain changes so much during the autumn with all the bracken that Kevin thought it might be a good idea if we went out again. Besides, there probably won't be many more weekends fine enough now that we're into November.'

'That's true,' Meg agreed, 'and once the snow comes to the high ground you'd be mad to try.'

Kate acknowledged the wisdom of her comment. Matt, like Kevin, was a member of their local rescue team, and both of them had heard enough from the men to be fully aware of the dangers awaiting the inexperienced foolish enough to venture out on to the Dales during the winter months.

'How did the dinner go, by the way?' Meg asked conversationally. 'I didn't get the opportunity to ask last night and on Wednesday I must have been asleep when you came in.'

Meg had been spending a couple of days up at

Matt's farm which they were busy decorating in preparation for their marriage in the summer, and Kate grimaced slightly. 'Oh, it wasn't so bad, although Rita made a big thing of suggesting that Kevin and I were lovers.'

'Oh no! But then that's typical of her,' Meg exclaimed. 'But tell me about her new man. Is he as gorgeous as she said?'

'He's certainly very handsome,' Kate agreed with a touch of acerbity, 'but handsome is as handsome does. If you want my real opinion, they're very well matched. Both of them are takers, if you know what I mean.'

'Umm. It seems the two of you didn't hit it off. Now that's funny,' Meg mused with a grin. 'Mary was in here yesterday choosing a sweater—Alan's promised to buy her one for Christmas, apparently. She said that our new Director of Operations couldn't keep his eyes off you.'

'Oh, you know Mary,' Kate said weakly. 'She dislikes Rita so much she tends to let her imagination run away with her.'

'But he did follow you out into the kitchen when Rita upset you,' Meg pressed.

Inwardly fuming, cursing Mary's too sharp eyes and too ready tongue, Kate said lightly, 'I suppose he thought it only good manners, although I wasn't actually on my own. I was with Lisa. You've got fifteen minutes before Matt arrives,' she reminded her friend. 'If you stay here cross-questioning me much longer, you'll never be ready.'

When Meg had gone Kate went to her own room and dressed slowly in her fell-walking gear. It could be cold out on the fells, especially when the temperature dropped sharply as it had a habit of doing and she dressed warmly in thermal top and tights, both in a pretty pink and white candy stripe which hugged her body revealingly—a far cry from the old-fashioned 'combinations' from which the thermal underwear had been derived. On top she wore a thin checked shirt and a sweater plus a pair of heavy jeans. Her quilted parka with its fur-trimmed hood lay on the bed, and as she bent down to lace up the sturdy boots Kevin had insisted on her buying she heard the phone ring.

Every time she had heard it since that fatal dinner party her stomach had lurched. Each time she picked up the receiver she dreaded hearing Jake's voice. Some time they would have to talk, she hated the deceit she was practising on her friends, and besides, it was high time they talked about their divorce. With Jake openly squiring other women about he no longer had any reason to refuse to accede to it. Oh, her lawyer had told her that he could make her wait the full five years if he wished, but what was the point? Their marriage was over and she, for one, only wanted to cut away from the past completely—and how could she do that when she and Jake, while masquerading as perfect strangers, were in reality still man and wife?

She picked up the receiver with nervous fingers, expelling a faint sigh of relief when she heard Kevin's voice. 'Kate, I'm so sorry,' he apologised, 'but I'm going to have to cancel today. Laura Braithwaite's gone into labour. The midwife's already with her, but I'll have to stand by. She's insisting on having this baby at home, but I want to be on hand just in case there are any problems.'

'Don't worry about it,' Kate assured him.

'While you're on I ought to tell you that Jake has set

up a meeting at the station to look into the safety standards and I've been invited to attend.'

'Marvellous!' Kate knew she sounded less than sincere, but she didn't care. It seemed that all her friends were enthusing about Jake, and absurdly she felt like a small child excluded from a particularly exciting birthday party.

Kevin rang off, and she paced the flat moodily. Outside the sun shone pale golden yellow from an ice blue sky, and restlessness stirred in her blood like wine. She didn't want to spend the day indoors. She wanted to be outside, breathing in the cold, pure Dales air. Why shouldn't she go for her walk alone? She wouldn't go far. She hunted along the bookshelves until she found the book of local walks she had bought when she first came to the Dales. There was one that didn't look too arduous and wasn't too long, which looped round the Dale and brought her back into the village again. The book had been specifically written for keen walkers, and various small crosses marked the spots where shepherds' huts had been turned into emergency rest-halts. The walks were picked out in differing colours to indicate their varying degrees of hardship, and the one Kate had picked was one of the easier ones. The time set for the walk was three hours, which meant that she should be back before dusk. Picking up the sandwiches she had made and her thermos, Kate tucked them into the pockets of her parka and zipped it up.

Half an hour later she was congratulating herself on her decision as she forded a small sluggish stream and followed one of the ancient drystone walls up towards the top of the hill. From its summit she surveyed the village spread out below her, carefully checking her map, knowing from Kevin how easily it was to lose the right path along these upland tracks. The air was so cold and pure that it stung her lungs and Kate gulped great breaths of it, feeling the tension ease out of her as she walked steadily along the track, pacing herself carefully as Kevin had taught her. One of the first faults of the amateur was to walk too quickly too soon, thus exhausting himself, he had explained to her on their very first walk, and as she climbed higher and higher through the Dale Kate paused regularly to look down the way she had come and to study her map. Because she was on her own she had decided against any fell-walking, knowing that if she did slip and sprain her ankle she would be completely alone, but she was still glad of the warm protection of her thick clothes as the afternoon wore on and the air grew colder.

At first she told herself that the chill was due to the greater height at which she was walking, but every time she stopped to take her bearings she noticed that the wind seemed colder. At two o'clock she stopped in the shelter of a small dip, and found a smooth stone to sit on while she ate her lunch. An inquisitive sheep ambled across to investigate her, closely followed by other members of its flock. Across on the other side of the dale Kate watched a farmer and his dog working their sheep.

Sheepdog trials were one of the events of the Dales, and Kate thoroughly enjoyed going to watch these skilled animals cleverly manoeuvering their charges. Kevin had explained to her that the pups were often put in with an old ram, especially if they had a tendency to be boisterous, and that the dogs soon learned to mark down the leader of any flock and to control it through him.

The dog on the opposite hillside was obviously a young one, and Kate marvelled both at the patience of the farmer and the stamina of the dog as calls and whistles were repeated over and over again until the dog thoroughly understood the command. Owning a good working dog was essential to sheep farming, and Kate knew that these dogs were exported all over the world. She had been toying with the idea of getting a pup herself. Kevin had told her that since she wanted the dog as a pet she would have no trouble getting a bitch puppy from one of the farmers. 'Bitches are harder to work with because they're more emotional than dogs,' he had told her with a grin, but Kate had refused to respond to the bait.

A sudden gust of wind reminded her that she had been sitting down longer than she intended, and she shivered as she stood up, glancing behind her as she stepped out of the protection of the hollow and discovered that the sun had stopped shining. A glance over her shoulder showed her why. While she had been eating her lunch and watching the farmer with his dog a thin mist had started to creep down the hillside. Already the hills above her were blotted out completely, and she felt a tug of nervousness in the pit of her stomach. Too often she had heard tales of the unwary wandering from the path in the heavy mists that shrouded the hills, losing their way completely, sometimes falling to their deaths as they strayed too far. Kate looked at her watch. She had come more than half way, but the remainder of the walk was more rugged, with sheer escarpments falling away to her left. On a clear day the track was perfectly safe and afforded magnificent views of the surrounding scenery, but in a thick mist. . . .

Kate looked anxiously behind her. Was it her imagination, or had the mist increased in the short space of time since she first noticed it? If it became any thicker she would be a fool to continue her walk, because she could easily lose the track and fall. On the other hand, no one knew where she was, and warm though her clothing was, it was no protection against a cold night spent outside on the fells. That left only one alternative. She would have to turn back. But that meant climbing again into the mist which was definitely thickening and creeping towards her.

'Don't panic,' Kate warned herself, sitting down again and pulling out her booklet. If only she had left a message for Meg, or told Kevin what she was doing. The world was full of regretful 'if onlys', though, and thinking about what she ought to have done would get her absolutely nowhere.

As she studied her map, her heart sinking as she mentally recorded the distance she had to walk back, and the height to which it would take her, Kate noticed one of the small crosses indicating a shepherd's hut. Carefully she calculated the distance. It was less than a mile away, but it was uphill. Frowning, she studied the relief map thoroughly. Although the track was uphill, it was on level ground and marked by a stone wall. All she had to do was to find the wall and follow it upwards and it would take her right to the hut. Shivering clammily, Kate refolded her map. She had been right. The mist was thickening and not just that, the temperature was dropping rapidly. Her hair was already damp from the mist and her fingers icy cold. As she stood up the mist whirled and eddied mysteriously around her, making it impossible for her to see more than half a dozen paces in front of her. That decided it. She daren't risk the downward path with its sheer drop on one side, and it was far too risky to try and make her way back. No, she would have to find the hut, or risk suffering the effects of exposure by staying where she was until morning and hoping that the mist would have lifted. Once again studying the map, Kate made her way slowly and carefully to the wall that led to the hut. When she found it, she expelled her breath on a tautly relieved sigh, double checking her bearings, knowing all too well the dangers of making a mistake at this juncture. If she got the wrong wall now. . . . But she hadn't done, she was sure of that. A mile. That should take her about half an hour, say forty minutes in view of the mist. She looked at her watch carefully checking the time, and then firmly forbidding herself not to dwell on all the hazards ahead of her, she set off.

Half an hour later, soaked to the skin from the thighs down where the thick mist had penetrated her jeans, and been soaked up by the porous stuff, Kate was shivering from cold and fear. Her jeans felt like clammy leg irons against her chaffed flesh, only the thickness of her parka preventing her upper body from suffering the same fate. It was impossible to see further than the hand she was holding in front of her face. Everywhere she looked the mist whirled and eddied like a monstrous dervish, mocking her inability to penetrate its thick veil. Only the darkly grey presence of the wall to her right helped her to hold on to sanity. Thank God for Kevin and that wall, because without it she would never have believed she was travelling in the right direction and many, many times would have been tempted to turn and wander round in wider and wider circles, completely losing her sense of direction.

All the time she had been walking she had been gradually climbing, her legs aching with the strain placed on exhausted muscles, her breath coming in shivery gasps as she fought not to give in to the panic tugging insidiously at her mind. She had been walking for over forty minutes now and there was no sign of the hut. What if she *had* chosen the wrong wall . . . what if. . . . She was just forcing down the panicky thoughts when the hut loomed in front of her, a small grey box emerging from the mist, and tears of thankfulness poured down her face as she straightened and stared at it. Oh, thank God! She was barely aware of muttering the words as she stumbled and staggered towards the hut, automatically hugging the wall which had been her guide and protection. As she reached it, she realised how much the temperature had dropped as she moved away from the lee of the wall and felt the ice flecked mist against her skin.

The hut was a simple stone building, barely twelve foot square. Inside it would be equipped with enough kindling to light the fire, and a small stove run off butane gas together with some basic supplies of food. Kate knew this because Kevin had once told her, when he had first enlisted her help in raising money to equip these walking stations, and never again would she quibble about the work involved, she thought fervently as she found the door and pushed it open.

Two thoughts struck her at the same time. The first was that the hut was beautifully warm, and the second was that there was someone already in occupation. The fire had been lit and thick woollen socks and a pair of jeans were drying in front of it. She could smell something cooking—beans—and never had anything smelled so delicious. There was a certain sense of camaraderie in knowing she wasn't the only one in need of a haven from the weather, but the smile curving her lips died and shock stormed through her as the man with his back to her stood up and turned round.

'Jake! What. . . .' She felt herself sway, more with shock than anything else and then Jake's hands were biting into the tender flesh of her waist, his voice rough in her ear as he said angrily, 'Kate, what the devil. . . . You didn't follow me up here, did you?'

'Follow you?' Shock gave way to anger, scorn igniting sapphire flames in the depths of her eyes. 'Why on earth would I want to do that?' she demanded tautly. 'You're the last person I expected to see up here!' She missed the grim tightening of his mouth and the way his eyes became icily bleak as they surveyed her soaking jeans and exhausted, pale face.

'What are you doing here, then? Lost your way on a Sunday stroll, did you?'

'Kevin and I were going to go fell-walking, but he was called out on a case,' Kate told him tiredly, pulling off her gloves and stretching out her hands eagerly to the warmth of the flames. 'I decided to walk alone—I was dressed and ready when he phoned, but then the mist came down just after lunch. I knew it was too dangerous to continue, and just as hazardous to turn back, and then I realised I could probably make it up here. . . .'

'You've changed,' she heard Jake saying curtly behind her. 'The Kate I knew would have sat down and indulged in hysterics until someone came and found her.'

'The Kate you knew was twenty years old and knew very little about life. Don't forget you married her straight out of college,' Kate reminded him brittly, 'but time and experience has a way of changing everyone. I learned to manage on my own because I had to, Jake. If I'd stayed out on the fell and indulged in tears, by morning I'd have been suffering from exposure. Apart from which no one would be likely to find me as no one knows where I am.'

'Rather foolish, wasn't it?' he asked coldly. 'I thought one of the first tenets of walking was to let someone know where you are.'

'In normal circumstances, yes, but Meg is spending the night at Matt's, so she won't be worrying about where I am.'

'And Kevin? Won't he be worried when you don't get back tonight?'

'Kevin?' Kate stared at him, then flushed as she remembered Rita's innuendoes. 'What about Rita, does she know where you are?' she asked him, ignoring his question.

Jake ignored her comment as she had ignored his. 'Now that you are here, you'd better get out of those wet things,' he said tersely. 'Oh, come on, Kate,' he grated when she didn't make any move to obey him. 'You're not going all coy on me, are you? Remember I've seen it all before, and it didn't incite me to lust then. You've nothing to fear from me,' he added brutally. 'I never did like women who used sex as a weapon.'

'I didn't!' Kate objected hotly. 'I. . . .'

'You refused to sleep with me,' Jake overruled her flatly. 'You refused to have my child.'

'Because I couldn't bear to bring a child into what you and men like you have made of the world! Death, destruction, pain. . . .'

'All those things were there before, Kate,' Jake told
her, and it seemed to Kate that there was weariness as
well as impatience in his voice. 'If I'd had any other
job would it have been any different?' He shook his
head, his mouth curling sardonically, the flicker of the
flames lending the sharply hewn planes of his face a
demonic arrogance that chilled Kate as she watched
him. 'It wasn't my job you rejected, Kate, it was me. I
ought to have realised at the time that you were too
immature, that you'd absorbed too many of Lyla's
half-baked theories. . . .'

'Theories like male and female equality, you mean?'
Kate countered bitterly. 'That was something you
never believed in, was it, Jake? As far as you were
concerned, I was subservient to you ... your
woman. . . .'

'Not subservient,' he corrected sharply, 'but not
equal, at least not in the sense that you mean. You
can't make male and female equal, Kate, each has its
virtues and its vices, and we're made to complement
one another. I'm not doubting women's ability or
stamina, I never did, I just feel that for a woman to
succeed in a male-orientated world—and make no
mistake, that is what ours is—she has to make too
many sacrifices, too many compromises. A woman
with children and a career is always being torn apart
with guilt and dread. I've seen it happen, I'm not
saying it's right or even fair, but that's the way it is.
And you destroy yourselves. Take a woman like Rita,
for instance. If she was a man she'd be admired by her
own sex for her ruthless pursuit of her own desires
and gain, but because she's a woman her fellow
women dislike her for those very vices which would be
virtues in a man. Lyla taught you to expect perfection

from marriage because that was what she was always
looking for, but it doesn't exist, because human beings
aren't perfect. Nothing I did was right, you even
resented me for giving you sexual pleasure.'

'That's not true!' But even as she said the words,
Kate knew there was a kernel of truth in what he said.
It wasn't so much the pleasure they had shared which
she resented, but Jake's ability to arouse a need in her
body even though her mind disliked everything he was
and stood for.

'Anyway, none of it matters any more,' Kate said
tiredly. 'Our marriage is over and has been for two
years. Why won't you agree to a divorce?' she asked
him. 'My solicitor. . . .'

'Why do you think?' She glanced at his profile,
noting the hard thinness of his lips, the planes of his
face which emphasised the polished thrust of his
cheekbones. He looked leaner than she remembered,
tireder, but the thick black lashes still fanned his skin
with the vulnerability she remembered and which had
moved her to tenderness on so many occasions in the
past, that vulnerability so at odds with the man she
knew him to be. 'Because our marriage, such as it is,
offers you a measure of protection against other
women,' Kate said forthrightly, remembering what
her lawyer had said. 'Does Rita know you're married?'

'She knows I'm separated,' he said casually, 'As you
say, the legal tie between us affords me a bolt-hole in
times of need. But what about you, what does Kevin
think about the fact that you're still legally tied to
another man?'

'Kevin is a friend and nothing more,' Kate retorted
hotly.

'Oh, come on! I saw the way he looked when you

walked out of that bedroom. It was obvious that you had nothing on under that robe. I know the enticement your body offers, Kate, so don't try telling me that Kevin is immune to it.'

'Why not? Not ten minutes ago you were telling me that you were.'

'He doesn't know you like I do. Look, get those jeans off,' Jake instructed, suddenly changing the subject, 'they're soaking!'

They were, and Kate knew it was ridiculous to feel shy about undressing in front of him. After all, he knew her body as intimately as she knew it herself; he had awakened it to pleasure and had taught it to respond with mindless sensuality to his touch. But that was the trouble. Even now, disliking him, hating their enforced intimacy, Kate could feel her body's response to him; the tension coiling through her stomach, the heavy thud of her heart.

'What the devil's the matter with you now?' He stood up, frowning, and Kate held her breath, watching the firelight play on the strong, powerful lines of his body. Like her he had obviously been saturated by the mist and had taken off his jeans and socks. A thick quilted jacket lay in one corner of the room and he had removed his sweater, his plaid shirt doing little to conceal the masculine structure of his body; his thighs, tanned beneath their sprinkling of dark hair. Kate felt the blood rush to her face as she vividly remembered the feel of his thighs against her, the heated rasp of taut male flesh and muscle against the quivering softness of her body.

'Are you going to take them off, or do I have to do it for you?' The grim, soft words penetrated the fog of sensation clouding her mind. 'I've already told you,

you've nothing to fear from me, although I would have thought the experience you've gained during the years we've been apart would have taught you when a man desires you and when he doesn't.'

His words were like a slap in the face. He spoke so contemptuously and callously, as though it mattered little to him what she did or with whom, but then why should it? She didn't care in the slightest about him any more, did she?

As she eased off her jeans with trembling fingers, Kate kept her eyes averted from Jake's body. The feelings looking at him had aroused were still too near the surface, and still had the power to disturb her. Who would ever have thought she would react to him like that? During their marriage she had wanted him, but she had always been content for him to take the initiative, she could never remember touching him without express invitation, whereas just then. . . . What on earth was she thinking of? She had *not* wanted to touch Jake, why should she? She hadn't desired any man in the years they had been apart, and she didn't want to. Desire was a treacherous trap designed to fog the mind and deceive the senses, and it was one she was going to avoid for the rest of her life.

'And those,' Jake said grimly, reaching out to curl his hand round her ankle to test the dryness of her tights, once she had removed her jeans. 'They're soaking as well. We can't leave here until morning, even if the mist does lift before then, and when we do leave it might as well be wearing dry clothes. There's a couple of sleeping bags here, so at least we should be able to sleep in comfort.' He had turned his back towards her and Kate pulled off her wet tights, watching the movements of his dark head, wondering at the aching hunger spreading through her lower body. By the time she had removed her tights and parka she had herself under control, shaken by the depth of need that had suddenly sprung to life inside her from a source she hadn't known existed. It was simply because they had once been lovers, she told herself shakily, a physical response to the past, intensified by the fact that there had been no other man in her life.

They ate their beans in silence, drinking the tea Kate brewed on the small stove. The hut was pleasantly warm, and her jeans were steaming in front of the fire. A pleasant lethargy invaded her body, disappearing as she moved and winced at the pain lancing through her skin.

'What's wrong?' Jake frowned, following the movement of her fingers along her inner thigh. The flesh was sore and chafed from her damp jeans and Kate winced again as her fingers brushed it.

'It's nothing,' she lied briefly. 'If you don't mind, Jake, I think I'll turn in.'

'Let me see,' he ordered, ignoring the final part of her sentence, and before she could stop him, his fingers were investigating the sore place discovered by her own.

'Nothing?' His eyebrows lifted in sardonic mockery as she flinched beneath his touch. 'My jeans were new and they rubbed. . . .'

'So I see. I've got some cream that might help.' He got up and walked across to his parka, while Kate sat still watching him. Her breath seemed to have lodged somewhere in her throat and she felt too weak to protest when, instead of handing her the tube, he kneeled down in front of her, uncapping it and

squeezing some lotion on to his fingers. It felt
wonderfully cool against her heated skin, but her
initial relief was swiftly followed by other and far more
disturbing sensations. The movement of Jake's fingers
against her skin sent feelings spiralling through her,
then rang alarm bells in her brain, the effort of
controlling her breathing so that she didn't betray the
effect he was having on her, draining the last fragile
resources of her control. But some responses couldn't
be controlled, and to her chagrin Kate felt the
unmistakable hardening of her nipples beneath the
thin fabric of her thermal top, and what was worse she
knew Jake was aware of it too, as he raised his head
slowly, the colour burning hotly in her face as his eyes
rested coolly on the aroused outline of her breasts. She
expected him to mock her and waited, with held
breath, for the scornful words that could only add to
her humiliation, her eyes closed defensively against the
expression she was sure she would see in the cold grey
depths of Jake's.

'Kate!' She heard him mutter her name, but nothing
could have prepared her for the fingers that probed
the tender outline of her breast, tugging at the candy-
striped fabric, until the pale flesh with its rosy
betraying aureole was exposed to his gaze. And not
just his gaze, Kate acknowledged on a shudder as the
hard pad of Jake's thumb brushed against her aroused
flesh. Her eyes flew open in stunned disbelief,
widening as they took in the dull, hectic flush of
colour staining the high cheekbones, and the liquid
intensity of the grey eyes that searched her face, before
returning avidly to her body. She was incapable of
protest when Jake bent over her and removed her top
completely, incapable of anything but amazed in-

credulity at the hunger she had never suspected she
had felt, but which was apparent in the starved
response of her body to his open appraisal. A
sensuality she had never known she possessed held her
still beneath Jake's slow inspection, only the slight
arching of her body as his hands moved slowly
downwards, cupping her breasts and lingering over
their softness, betraying the fierce need that had come
leaping to live inside her the moment he touched her.

'Kate ... Kate, I'm so damned hungry for you,'
Kate heard him mutter, and then his mouth was on
hers, blotting out the protest she would have made,
invading and possessing the moist inner sweetness
until a familiar languor started to sweep over her. Her
lips admitted the probing heat of his, her fingers
twining in his hair to hold him against her when he
lifted his head, his tongue moistening the delicate
shaping of her ear, his teeth tugging softly, nipping
her tingling flesh. Her hands had found their way
inside his shirt, her palms flat against the moist heat of
his chest, her lips pressing tiny, hungry kisses against
his throat, tasting its masculine texture. The past,
their separation, all were forgotten, there was only
Jake now, and the tumultuous feelings he aroused
inside her, feelings that were now clamouring for
release. She ached to touch and caress him, to feel his
body shudder in pleasure against hers.

'Kate, you're as hungry as I am,' Jake groaned
against her ear, nibbling the sensitive flesh. 'The
lovers you've had since we've been apart can't have
known how to please you, my Cat.' His hand stroked
smoothly down her body, every vibrant pulse leaping
to life, but his words chilled her heated flesh,
reminding her of who he was and all that lay between

them; for a moment she lay still, listening to the siren song of her body, knowing how much it craved Jake's touch, but her mind reminded her of all the pain and misery she had endured through this man.

'If you're hungry, Jake, I suggest you tell Rita,' she managed to say coolly as she pulled away from him.

An expletive that made her shrink splintered the silence, and Kate quailed beneath the look of bitter loathing he gave her. 'I'd forgotten that was always one of your favourite games, Kate,' he told her savagely as he stood up, 'but it's a game you can't always play without getting burned. If I lie there aching for satisfaction tonight, at least I'll have the compensation of knowing you're aching too. I thought when I saw you the other night that you'd finally grown up, but I was wrong—you're still the same little fool you always were.' He reached for one of the rolled-up sleeping bags and tossed it over to her. 'Sweet dreams,' he gritted unpleasantly, turning his back on her as he pulled out the second sleeping bag and carefully banked up the fire, until it was little more than a glow, but as she had been dangerously reminded tonight, even the dimmest embers could be whipped into a burning inferno, given the right conditions. How could she have desired him? Shivering, she slid into the quilted bag. It was no use pretending, she *had* desired him, and with an intensity that made her shake uncontrollably as she tried to calm herself enough to go to sleep. If she hadn't made that remark, by now. . . . She shuddered and resolutely closed her eyes. She had done the right thing. She couldn't have faced herself if she had encouraged Jake to make love to her. The only reason he had wanted her was to appease his need. A man like Jake could never live like a monk. Like her, he had been affected by their intimacy, by memories of their marriage. Thank God she had stopped him when she had.

CHAPTER FOUR

MUCH to Kate's chagrin Jake had insisted on accompanying her back to Woolerton, and of course their arrival together didn't go unnoticed. While Meg and Kevin accepted her explanation of how they had come to find themselves together at the hut, without any comment other than merely remarking on the coincidence, Kate discovered that Rita put a very different interpretation on the situation.

She arrived at the shop just as Kate was about to stop for her coffee break, her blue eyes glittering with malice, her face flushed with anger.

'I suppose you think you've been very clever,' was her opening remark, 'but Jake is far too intelligent to be taken in by you. It's obvious that you've been trying to gain his attention from the first time you saw him, but it won't work, Kate. So I'm warning you now. . . .' she broke off as the shop door bell rang, and Kate didn't know which of them was the more astounded when Jake himself walked in. Rita gave Kate a murderous glance before linking her arm through Jake's and cooing softly, 'Darling, how nice! Now you can drive me home—I wanted to see you anyway. Daddy always has a dinner party before the Hunt Ball, and of course you'll be included. What brings you here?' she added, giving Kate another angry glare. 'Don't tell me you want one of Kate's jumpers!'

'I was passing by and I came to see how you

were,' Jake addressed the comment to Kate, ignoring Rita, who was still clinging to his arm, looking furious.

'Fine,' Kate assured him brittly. 'And you?'

'I think I'll survive—I've endured worse in the past,' and for some reason the sardonic remark made Kate think, not of the mist and their danger, but of danger of another kind, the sort she had experienced in his arms, and her cheeks grew hot as she wondered if he had deliberately steered her thoughts in that direction.

'Personally I can't think what you were doing out on the fells,' Rita interrupted, eyeing Kate angrily.

She wasn't going to be drawn into an argument with the other woman, Kate decided, counting ten mentally as she held back the words clamouring for utterance. Out of the corner of her eyes she could see that Jake was watching her curiously. Three years ago when they had first met, someone like Rita would have terrorised her, but the intervening months had brought a measure of maturity and self-confidence that enabled her to cope with Rita's jealous insinuations.

'Phew! What brought that on?' Meg enquired when Jake and Rita had left. 'I heard it all from the storeroom.'

'Rita seems to think—quite erroneously—that I'm out to snatch Jake from under her nose.'

'Umm, I wouldn't blame you for trying,' Meg grinned. 'There's a man who's definitely all male,' she added appreciatively, 'but definitely not the type to let anyone else make his decisions for him. Has she got reason to be jealous?' she asked cautiously. 'I mean, he did come to see how you were?'

'Not as far as I'm concerned,' Kate responded coolly. 'Like I've already said, he's not my type.'

'Yes, I know you've said it,' Meg agreed. 'That's what's worrying me!' She raised her eyebrows teasingly, and continued, 'Kate, he's every woman's secret type, and well you know it.'

'I'll tell Matt,' Kate threatened, but inwardly she was aching with pain. Meg was right, Jake had sex appeal that few women could resist. During their brief marriage she had nearly been driven insane by jealousy every time another woman looked at him, which was almost continually. They had had bitter rows about it, although she had always masked the true cause of her anger, which was her fear that he might turn away from her to one of these other women. Right from the start she had doubted her own ability to hold him. Even though she had loved him with an intensity that shook her to the heart, she had never told him. He had married her on some whim because he thought she was vulnerable and because he disapproved of Lyla's influence over her; he had told her she was so sexually responsive to him that their marriage couldn't help but be a success, but he had said it with an undertone of cynicism, she recognised now, and he had never said that he loved her, never once. He had wanted her, he had desired her physically and in those first early months had seemed to derive a savage satisfaction from making her respond just as ardently to him, but love had been a word neither of them had ever uttered.

So their marriage had been a mistake, Kate thought angrily as she started to tidy up the shelves. So what was new? She had known that within six months of marrying him, although she had tried to make it work.

Jake had been the one who left, the one who threw out that taunting, 'Come and find me when you're finally grown up.'

By mid-afternoon she felt so restless that she knew she would have to escape the confines of the shop and expel some of her nervous action in physical activity. Leaving Meg alone, she set off in the direction of Little Cottage.

It was another cold day and the east wind knifed through her wool jacket as she hurried through the village. Sarah welcomed her warmly, opening the door almost before she knocked. 'I saw you coming down the street,' she beamed. 'Have you got time for a cup of tea?'

As she bustled about her small kitchen Kate watched her affectionately. She was talking over her shoulder to Kate about the power station, explaining that one of her nieces had just got a job there. 'Aye, I know you're against it, Kate,' she agreed when she had poured them both a cup of tea, 'but there's a lot of folk round here grateful for the jobs it gives them.' She frowned suddenly and went pale as someone knocked on the door.

'I'll get it for you, shall I?' Kate offered, as she was nearest. For a moment Sarah had looked quite ill, and Kate frowned. Her friend was well into her seventies and although she always looked fit and healthy perhaps she was more frail than Kate had imagined. As she opened the door, she was forced to take a step back as the youth who stood there pushed open the door, lounging there in a manner that was somehow threatening, although he couldn't have been more than fifteen.

'See you've got a visitor,' he commented laconically

to Sarah, who was standing behind Kate. 'I'll call round later, then.'

'He's a nephew of Mrs James's,' Sarah explained when he had gone. 'He comes round sometimes to run errands and do little jobs. . . .' Her voice sounded unusually breathless and Kate could have sworn she saw fear in the older woman's eyes for a moment, but she changed the subject so swiftly that Kate felt it would be impolite to pry. By the time she got up to leave she had managed to convince herself that she must have imagined that brief flash of fear in the faded blue eyes when they rested on Mrs James's nephew, but even so she turned impulsively at the door to hug the old lady. 'You know you can always come to me if . . . if . . . you need someone to talk to, don't you?'

'You're a fine lassie,' Sarah told her warmly. 'I'll have yon jumper finished by the end of the month. Mind how you go now, that wind's bitter cold.'

Kate was halfway down the street when an imperative hoot on a car horn sounded behind her, making her turn automatically just in time to see Jake pulling alongside her in a gleaming black BMW.

'Get in,' he instructed curtly. 'I'll give you a lift—you look frozen. Don't waste time arguing, Kate,' he continued when she hesitated, 'get in.'

For some reason she couldn't later define, Kate did as he instructed, dismayed to discover how much she quivered inwardly as she fastened her seat-belt and tried to relax. It was only a matter of a quarter of a mile or so to the shop, but over every yard of it she was intensely conscious of Jake at her side, his hands lean and sure as he manoeuvred the powerful car, the fabric of his business suit stretched tautly across his thighs as he drove and the intimacy of the car which seemed to enfold her in a web of tension.

'No after-effects from the other night?'

Kate darted a glance at him, moistening dry lips with her tongue as she probed the words carefully for a hidden meaning. 'None at all,' she assured him coolly, 'but then when one keeps a cool head and acts logically instead of giving in to panic, there seldom is.'

Now let him ponder on her words! 'We're here,' she added calmly. 'Thank you for the lift.' She was reaching for the handle as he stopped, but his fingers on her sleeve stopped her. 'Don't forget to save me a dance at the Hunt Ball,' he told her softly, watching her shiver under the faint threat laced through the words. 'We've got a lot of news to catch up on, and. . . .'

'I won't be used by you to make Rita jealous, Jake,' Kate told him emphatically, 'and the only thing I want from you is my divorce. Our marriage was a farce, and. . . .'

'I couldn't agree more.' The curt, clipped tones silenced her for a moment, and she blinked uncertainly at him as he leaned forward and across her, releasing the catch on the door. As he made to withdraw Kate moved forward, the brief movement bringing her breasts in contact with the hard warmth of his arm, her skin tingling beneath her clothes, her lungs tortured with lack of oxygen as she held her breath stunned by the tumult of her senses. Memories long dormant flared to life, her body intensely aware of the man seated beside her, feelings and desires she had relentlessly subdued since she left him bursting through the barriers she had erected against them. When she got out of the car she wasn't surprised to discover that her legs could barely support her. It had been like this when she first knew him. He only had to look at her and she melted. But that was then. Now she ought to be immune to the traitorous surge of her senses. She ought to be, but she wasn't, Kate admitted grimly when she had closed the door behind her, leaning against it while she tried to gather her distracted thoughts. What she was suffering from was plain old-fashioned frustration, she told herself bluntly. Since Jake there had been no one, unless she counted the almost brotherly kisses she had shared with Kevin, and perhaps it was only natural that seeing him should re-awaken all those feelings she had thought dead.

'Meg, what do you think?' Anxiously Kate peered in the mirror, examining her reflection. The Hunt Ball was the highlight of the local social calendar and the dress she had bought for it was one that she would not normally have worn. The time she had spent with Lyla had reinforced her own natural good taste, and now with the business so successful she had the money to indulge herself in the odd luxury, which this gown—there was surely no other word to describe it— most certainly was.

It was a copy of a Dior model and she had bought it in Paris. Made of purest cream silk crêpe, it clung softly to her body, the padded shoulders and dolman sleeves emphasising the slenderness of her waist and hips. Throat high at the front, at the back it bared her body to her waist, before falling in a straight swathe to her feet. For once her hair was piled up on top of her head in a cluster of soft curls, pearl and diamond drop earrings and matching choker being the only jewellery she was wearing.

'Meg?' She glanced anxiously at her friend when there was no response. 'It's all wrong, isn't it?' she agonised. 'I ought to have bought something in taffeta with a huge skirt and. . . .'

'Wrong? It's stunning!' Meg told her breathlessly. 'Oh Kate, you look . . . fantastic! Like an ice princess, remote and beautiful in an ivory tower. It must have cost the earth.'

'It did,' Kate agreed ruefully. 'Nearly all my bonus and Lyla's birthday cheque.'

'Then you must want to impress someone,' Meg slipped in slyly, 'and something tells me it's going to be wasted on Kevin!'

'Perhaps I just want to prove that being anti-nuclear weapons doesn't necessarily go hand in hand with jeans and austerity,' Kate responded, knowing nevertheless that she had coloured faintly. She had bought the dress long before Jake had appeared in the village, but she was too honest with herself to deny that his presence had contributed to her decision to wear it. And why not? Why shouldn't she show him the woman she had become? Especially when he continually flaunted Rita in front of her eyes—or rather Rita flaunted him. She had made it plain that she had laid claim to Jake in no uncertain terms, and there was already gossip in the village about the possibility of their marriage. Rita obviously didn't know about *her*, Kate reflected wryly as she slipped on her fox jacket and picked up her satin purse. Kevin had promised to collect her and drive her to the ball, which was being held in a large country house ten miles outside the village, which was owned by the National Trust and which the Hunt Ball Committee always rented for the occasion.

When Kevin didn't arrive at the appointed time, Kate glanced hesitantly at the phone. He had probably been called out somewhere, which meant she would have to go by taxi. 'Don't panic,' Meg called out from her bedroom. 'I hear a car.' Her pronouncement was followed in seconds by a ring on the bell and Kate hurried to open the door. 'Kevin! I was just beginning to think you'd been called out.'

'Come on in Kevin,' Meg called out behind her. 'Wait until you see Kate's finery—she looks stunning!' Both of them fell silent as they realised their mistake. It wasn't Kevin who stood outside the door but Jake, his mouth quirking in wry amusement when he saw their expressions.

'You really know how to boost a man's ego, don't you?' he mocked, but it was on Kate that his eyes lingered, the cold, bitter message in their grey depths making her shiver deep inside.

'Oh, Jake, we were expecting Kevin,' Meg explained unnecessarily. 'Has. . . .'

'You were right first time,' Jake drawled, walking into the room, his words for Meg, but his eyes on Kate, examining the slender length of her until she felt as though her skin burned under the lash of his gaze. 'Kevin has been called out—he'll be delayed, and he asked me to pick you up, Kate.'

'But I thought you were dining with Rita and her parents beforehand?'

'I couldn't make it.' His tone forbade any further questions. 'If you're ready?'

Suppressing a cowardly inclination to refuse to go with him, Kate said her goodbyes to Meg, and preceded Jake through the door. They walked in silence to the car. Jake opened the door for her, settling her comfortably inside before he closed it, and then walked round to the driver's side. The car was set in motion before he glanced at her again, and Kate hoped that none of the churning emotions inside her were visible in her face. What was wrong with her? she wondered. After all, she had travelled with him like this before. No, never, quite like this she admitted darting a glance at his impassive face, acknowledging that formal clothes suited him. They hadn't gone out much together during their marriage. Oh, they had been invited out often enough—friends and colleagues of Jake's, but she had always refused to go; to collaborate with the enemy, she remembered once terming a dinner party they had been invited to. A faint sigh escaped softly parted lips. Had she really been so childish? She had learned a good deal in three years, including tolerance. Since coming to Woolerton she had met the ex-head of the station and his wife on several occasions socially and had found them a pleasant couple, although that had not detracted one iota from her dislike of what he stood for.

'Quite like old times. . . .' Jake drawled, and then corrected himself mockingly, 'Oh, no—I forgot, you always refused to go to affairs like this with me, didn't you? You claimed you detested the people I worked with—not that you actually ever met any of them. My boss once asked me if you were a semi-invalid, I remember.'

In the darkness of the car Kate felt safe enough to stare at him, realising for the first time how embarrassing her behaviour must have been to him.

'What did you tell him?' she asked curiously,

furious with herself the moment the words were uttered.

'That you suffered from an over-acute social conscience,' Jake told her dryly. 'Oh, you weren't on your own. It was quite fashionable at the time, if I remember rightly, for the younger wives to be anti their husbands' jobs.'

'It must have been embarrassing for you.' She was doing no more than speak her thoughts aloud, but in the darkness she felt Jake drop the speed of the car to turn and glance at her.

'Wasn't that the whole object of the exercise?' he asked sardonically, 'to cause me as much embarrassment as possible—so much that I'd give up the job I'd worked ten years to get?'

Kate was honestly perplexed. She had wanted him to give up his job, of course, and had, on more than one occasion, begged him to do so, but she had never thought of using her own behaviour to force him to do so. 'No.' Her answer was instantaneous.

'Oh? Then what was the purpose of it?'

She bit her lip. How could she admit that she hadn't even thought before her own bitter hatred of what he was doing; her own code of ethics and morals which had told her that socialising with Jake's colleagues would be betraying her cause.

'Well, it worked in the end, anyway,' Jake told her laconically. 'A man can only stand being made to feel guilty for everything he does for so long. Every time I so much as touched you your eyes reproached me. In the end I felt as though I were making you break some sacred vow every time I came near you, but I've never given in to blackmail, Kate, and I wasn't about to start with you, much as I. . . .' He bit off whatever he had been about to say and added cruelly, 'I'd seen the results of giving in to female caprice in my father. Lyla destroyed him as a man and then when she was bored with him she divorced him. I swore that would never happen to me. You wanted me to give up my job, and you used every trick in the book to make me.'

'No!' Kate recognised the pain in her denial, and bit her lip in the darkness, hoping Jake hadn't heard it too. 'Well, like you I have my pride,' Jake told her smoothly, 'and like I said, I wasn't going to give in to blackmail.'

Was that why he hadn't dined with Rita and her parents? Kate wondered thoughtfully. It was obvious to Kate that Rita was the one setting the pace of their relationship, and Jake would resent that. 'Does Rita know we're married?' she asked him curiously. Again she felt the car decrease in speed as he turned towards her.

'No. Why should she?'

'She was very unpleasant about that night we spent in the shepherd's hut. She seemed to think I'd engineered it deliberately, she warned me that she had a prior claim on you.' Kate didn't know why she was pursuing his relationship with Rita. She wasn't a fool, Rita wouldn't have been the only woman in his life during the time they had been apart and she had never given either them or him a thought. Of course it was one thing to know that it was happening, it was quite another to be forced to watch it.

'You could always tell her the truth,' Kate almost gasped her astonishment aloud, as Jake slashed a mocking glance in her direction, watching her reaction.

So her solicitor had been right, Jake was using their

marriage as a form of protection. 'What truth?' Kate asked, managing to keep her voice level. 'That we were married and that our marriage is now over? Why won't you agree to a divorce, Jake? You don't want me, I don't want you.'

'It isn't something we can talk about right now.'

'But we can discuss it.'

'Yes.' His voice sounded terse. 'I've rented a house just outside Woolerton.' He described it to her and Kate recognised it as belonging to a couple who had gone out for two years to the Middle East where the husband had a job. 'I'm free on Saturday, why don't you come round then and we can discuss it?'

It seemed a reasonable suggestion, so why did she have this nerve-racking feeling that somehow she was stepping off a safe path into dangerously unsafe territory?

'It will have to be after we close the shop,' she temporised. 'Meg normally goes up to the farm to see Matt on Saturday.'

'Okay. Tell me what time you close and I'll come and pick you up.'

It was only after they had made the arrangements that Kate realised she could just as easily have suggested they talk on her home ground, but it was too late to change the details now without alerting Jake to the fact that she felt uneasy with him, and he already had the balance weighted too much in his favour for her to give him any more advantages.

When they arrived at their destination the forecourt in front of the house was already half full of cars. Kate recognised Rita's father's Rolls, and her heart sank a little as she contemplated Rita's reaction to discovering she had arrived with Jake. She dawdled deliberately in the cloakroom hoping he would lose patience and go in without her, but when she emerged he was lounging against the wall, arms folded across his chest.

'That's something new,' he murmured when she rejoined him. 'I always used to think you didn't spend hours titivating yourself because you couldn't bear to be away from me.'

'At twenty-one one doesn't need to spend the same amount of time on one's appearance as one does at twenty-four,' Kate told him coolly.

He made no response, but there was a definite gleam of mockery in his eyes as he surveyed her slowly from head to foot. His attention was directed to her face when he asked casually. 'Am I right in thinking that this . . .' he touched the silk draping one shoulder briefly, 'is all that comes between you and your skin?'

The question was so unexpected that she flushed darkly and betrayingly, gritting her teeth at his genuine laughter over her embarrassment. 'Umm, knowing that will make me enjoy our dance together all the more,' he murmured against her ear, his palm resting on the smooth skin of her back as they walked towards the double doors leading into the ballroom. 'That's something else you've learned in the time we've been apart. I seem to remember I had to coax you to wear anything other than the most prim and proper clothes, and you'd only let me undress you in the dark.'

It was true, but now was hardly the place to discuss it, Kate seethed inwardly. 'Do go on, your conversation tonight is most edifying,' she lied. 'How many other faults have you listed against me?'

'Nothing like as many as you have listed against me I'm sure, and I'll say one thing for you, when I did manage to coax you out of your virginal modesty, the results were . . . er . . . extremely gratifying.'

'More gratifying than those you've achieved with Rita?' Anger had turned her eyes as dark as sapphires, but Kate was unaware of the rage burning deep in their depths as chagrin touched her skin pink as she realised the danger of her question.

For a moment something strange glinted across the cool greyness of Jake's gaze. 'Why, Kate,' he said softly, 'are you trying to tell me you're jealous, my little Cat? Comparisons, as you must know, are odious, so we're told, but if it makes you feel any better, then I will admit that given the differing raw material, then yes—although spectacular would be the word I'd choose rather than gratifying. You used to go up like dry tinder when I touched you, however much you protested beforehand. Do you remember? I only had to kiss you and. . . .'

His voice was having a peculiarly mesmerising effect upon her, strange sensations shooting through her almost like pains as though something struggled for survival inside her. Her mouth had gone dry, her tongue touching nervously against her lips. As they spoke Jake had drawn her into a shadowy corner, his back blocking her from anyone else's view. His eyes followed the brief betraying movement of her tongue and he moved, palms resting flat aginst the wall either side of her, his body close, but not quite touching hers, until every nerve ending was agonisingly aware of him, and she could see the pores of his skin, the clean-shaven line of his jaw which would darken shortly, and which rasped her delicate skin when he touched her. He moved, bending his head, his tongue flicking lightly against her lips until they trembled weakly beneath the sensual lash, an enervating heat draining all the strength and resistance from her body.

'You lied to me earlier on,' Jake murmured against her mouth. His voice broke the spell which had mesmerised her, and reality impinged on the dream state she seemed to have entered, her body quivering uncontrollably as she became conscious of the heat coming off Jake's, wrapping her in a sensual awareness of him.

'I. . . . What do you mean?' Her voice sounded husky and unfamiliar and automatically she followed Jake's glance down her body as he moved away from her. Beneath the cream crêpe her nipples were outlined in explicit detail, thrusting against the rich material, as though deliberately enticing his gaze, and hot colour stormed her face as Jake drawled, 'You said you didn't want me, but I say you do, don't you, Kate?' And his laughter filled her ears, hateful and mocking as he led her towards the double doors again.

Rita pounced on him almost the moment they were inside, and she must have been watching for him, Kate decided, stunned by the fierce piercing sense of dislike she felt towards the other girl as she curled her fingers round his arm.

'Darling, at last . . . I thought you'd got lost!' She darted a bitter glare towards Kate. 'Where's Kevin? I thought he was bringing you?'

'He had a call,' Jake explained, 'so I volunteered to pick her up . . . not that there was much sacrifice involved,' he added lazily, letting his glance slide potently over her body, until Kate could almost feel the hatred Rita was directing towards her. Was this Jake's way of letting Rita know that she was getting too possessive? If so, she wanted no part of it, Kate decided sickly, excusing herself to go and speak to some friends.

Kevin arrived halfway through the evening, full of apologies, but just in time to take her in to supper. Kate hadn't seen him for some time and they had a lot to catch up on. A meeting with Jake and his colleagues had been set before Christmas, Kevin told her, reminding her that she had promised to take notes for him. 'I can't always remember what's been said, so it would be a terrific help if you could. . . .'

'If she could what?' Jake asked, suddenly materialising at their side, Rita still in tow.

'Oh, I was just telling Kate when the meeting of the Safety Committee's been set for. She's coming with me to take notes.'

'Only if she promises not to blow the place up while she's there,' Jake intervened. Rita laughed unkindly, and Kate responded,

'Oh, I'll promise not to cause havoc!'

They all laughed, but Jake bent his head and murmured softly, 'That, my little Cat, is something you do as a matter of course.' His eyes were on her breasts and Kate hated the way she flushed, knowing that Jake was mocking her by suggesting, as he had done, that she affected him sexually. Even at those times when she had been most responsive she had sensed a holding back in him, a control.

He came to claim his dance while Kevin was talking to Alan and Mary. Almost typically the music changed the moment he led her on to the floor, the slow seductive throb finding an answering beat in her own body. She deliberately held herself away from him, and watched his eyebrows rise tauntingly. 'What's the matter? You've danced with me before.'

'This isn't dancing,' Kate protested as his hands slid down her back, imprisoning her against him, the hard muscles of his thighs pressing against her as he deliberately reinforced their intimacy.

'No, then what is it?'

'It's. . . .' How could she say what was in her mind? That Jake was deliberately tantalising and arousing her; and he was succeeding, she acknowledged bitterly; her body was responding to the sensual brush of his like a flower in the desert beneath a sudden shower of rain. She had to fight not to melt against him, not to let her hands slide inside his jacket and investigate the warm, moist flesh beneath his shirt. His heart thudded unevenly against her almost as though it was trying to force its way inside her body, and the movement of Jake's hands over her back was so blatantly sensual that she could feel her breasts swelling and hardening in response, the pit of her stomach a raging ache of need that horrified her in its unexpectedness. She had never felt like this before. Oh, she had wanted his kisses, his caresses, but only when he was making love to her, and never with this savage hunger that most of her mind shrank from but that a corner was brave enough to investigate, and acknowledge that nothing would give her more satisfaction right now than for him to make love to her.

'No!' The word whispered past her numb lips, her eyes widening in disbelief, as she missed a beat and stumbled against him.

The instant she felt the hard pressure of his body as his arms tightened round her, Kate knew that she wasn't alone in her desire. As though he read her mind Jake confirmed roughly, 'Right now there's nothing I want more than to take you home with me, take off this damned dress and make love to you until there isn't a thought in your head that doesn't include me, but that's my body speaking to me, my mind tells me a different story; like it's time I returned you to your date.'

'So that you can return to yours? I'm sure Rita will prove amply accommodating,' she told him nastily, hating herself for the bitchy comment, but unable to stop herself from uttering it. Frustration was a powerful stimulant, she acknowledged unhappily, and it wasn't something she was used to experiencing.

'And far less troublesome,' Jake agreed, watching her narrowly. 'You were never simply content with what we had, were you, Kate? But was it necessary to go and destroy it completely?'

She wasn't given the opportunity to reply. The music stopped and he marched her back to their table, leaving her with Kevin while he returned to Rita.

The rest of the evening passed in a blur. Kate saw him leave with Rita less than an hour later and for the rest of the night her imagination tortured her with images of them together. Would he touch and caress Rita as he had once done her, making love to her with a skill that defied resistance; that swept aside all barriers and reduced the woman in his arms to an eager pliant responsiveness? Sickened by the ferocity of the jealousy that consumed her, Kate tried to block out the images. What was the matter with her? Why was she so jealous?

All in all she was glad when the evening was over, although she couldn't help glancing down the lane which led to the house Jake was renting when Kevin drove her past it. No lights were on, and she wondered bitterly if Rita too preferred making love in the dark.

CHAPTER FIVE

KATE was just nervously smoothing the skirt of her velvet suit when she heard the doorbell, and although her ears had been alert for the sound she still jumped nervously.

The afternoon was already fading into murky evening, the unpleasantness of the weather apparent as she opened the door to Jake. He seemed to loom up out of the darkness, taller and broader in the flesh than he appeared in her thoughts.

'Ready?'

Numbly she nodded her head, picking up her bag and checking that she had her key. As they stepped out into the street she noticed the youth staring at Jake's car and recognised him as the same boy she had seen at Sarah's cottage. He had a sullen, dangerous expression and something in the way he looked at her brought her skin out in goosebumps. She tensed and moved instinctively closer to Jake, who was watching the boy with thin-lipped anger. 'Do you know him?' he asked as he unlocked her door for her.

'Not really. He called round to see a friend of mine when I was there last. He does odd jobs for her.'

'Umm. You surprise me, he doesn't look the type who would do anyone a favour for nothing.' His words only confirmed Kate's own views, but she was too wrought up about their coming discussion to take the matter further.

'Jake, do we have to go to your house?' she asked

huskily when he was in the car. 'Couldn't we just sit here and. . . .'

'We could, but we're not going to. I'm cold and tired, Kate, it's been one hell of a long week and although you may not have noticed it this seat isn't exactly an armchair. Besides, I'm hungry and I asked Mrs Hillary, my daily, to leave some food for us.'

'She knows that I . . . that we. . . .'

'That you're having dinner with me?' he finished for her, eyebrows lifting slightly as she stumbled over the words. 'Yes, she knows, is there any reason why she shouldn't? Or are you worried that Kevin might get the wrong impression?'

'Kevin and I are just friends and. . . .'

'Not lovers,' he interrupted without looking at her, the cool amusement in his voice bringing her glance sharply to his face. 'Poor man, he doesn't know what he's missing, nor is he likely to find out, I suspect.'

'You've changed your tune,' Kate responded sarcastically. 'It's barely a fortnight since you accused me of having a procession of lovers through my life since, since we split up.'

'Ah yes, but that was before you responded to me so hungrily, my little Cat; like a woman who's been starved of a lover's touch for much too long.' Why was he speaking to her like this? He had no right to, no right at all. Her fingers curled angrily into her palms as she searched for a weapon sufficiently powerful to stop him.

'My private life is nothing to do with you any more, Jake,' was the best she could manage, 'and I don't want to discuss it with you.'

'Has there been anyone since we parted, Kate?' he pressed, completely ignoring her comment.

'I don't want to talk about it. I don't question you about your personal life. All I want from you is. . . .'

'A divorce—yes, I know.' For a moment he almost sounded bitter, but as Kate stared at him he recovered his self-control and drawled lightly, 'All right, the subject of lovers is taboo.' He turned the car into the drive leading to his house. 'But don't expect me to treat you like a polite stranger, Kate. We've been lovers; man and wife, and there can't be any going back to the level of mere acquaintanceship.'

She was familiar enough with the house he was renting not to need direction to the pleasant living room. As she passed the small study she noticed that the desk was heaped with papers, and Jake's mouth compressed grimly as he followed the direction of her glance.

'Kevin was quite right to call for a meeting of the Safety Committee; a certain laxity about some aspects of personal safety seems to have crept into the station, and it's causing me a few headaches. I'm telling you that because you'll hear it anyway when you attend the meetings, but it is privileged information, Kate, you do understand that, don't you?'

Her face flushed angrily. What did he think she was going to do with his confidence? Announce it to the world at large? As it happened she was already aware of the deficiences at the station from various things Kevin had said to her, but it still hurt to know that Jake thought her petty-minded enough to take advantage of a comment made out of context.

'Sit down and I'll get you a drink before I check on our dinner,' he suggested, running his fingers tiredly through his hair, a gesture she recognised with an aching tug of pain. 'I had to call at the station this afternoon and my meeting ran on longer than I intended. Could you bear with me while I go and shower?'

'If you're feeling tired we can easily put off our talk until another time,' Kate suggested, not wanting to acknowledge the reaction of her body to the images conjured up by his words. She remembered that he had always liked to shower when he got home from work. In the early days of their marriage he had coaxed her into joining him, but later when she had begun to resent the dominance he had over her body, she had seen these pre-dinner sessions as just another attempt to subvert her will, and had curtly refused to join him. What surprised her most, though, was that instead of remembering the angry bitterness which had given her the determination to resist him then, all she could remember was the heady pleasure she had found in his arms, beneath his hands. . . . 'You don't have to give me dinner,' she concluded breathlessly.

'I don't have to,' he agreed, his mouth wry, 'but a pleasant meal and a glass of wine should put us both in a better frame of mind to talk things over without losing our tempers, don't you agree? I won't be long.'

Somehow his assumption of an intimacy between them which did not really exist unnerved her, and all the time he was gone Kate found herself growing increasingly tense. She had come here so that they could talk about their divorce like two mature adults, instead of which she felt as nervous and on edge as a teenager on her first date.

'Ready for another drink?' She gasped when she heard Jake's voice, even though she had been listening for it. He had changed into a thin white silk shirt, the fine fabric clinging lovingly to the powerful contours of his chest. Narrow, dark pants moulded the lean muscularity of his hips and thighs, and Kate discovered to her chagrin that she was trembling so much that she had to put her empty glass down on the coffee table.

The Hardings' house was slightly unusual in design in that the stairs went up from the living room rather than the small hall, and the galleried landing looked down on the comfortable family room below. Staring up at Jake as he walked to the head of the stairs had a restricting effect on her breathing. Suddenly she felt acutely selfconscious; intensely aware of his maleness and disturbed by her own entirely feminine reaction to it. She was behaving like a nervous virgin, she warned herself as he poured her a second glass of wine without waiting for her response—no, not that, she admitted on a briefly illuminating flash of self-knowledge, because she actually wanted Jake to touch her. The quivering sensation assailing her lower stomach was one of need and not fear. Her tensed muscles were locked in frustrated desire, not panic. . . .

'Kate?' She moved awkwardly when he spoke her name, reaching blindly for the glass in his hand and missing it, and the contents soaked through her silk blouse and expensive skirt. Her reactions to the mishap were intensified by the knowledge that she had been too blinded by sexual desire for him to know what she was doing and she jumped up in shock, dabbing uselessly at the soaking fabric, bright spots of colour burning in her cheeks, as the dark red stain seeped into the fragile silk and velvet.

'Quick, take them off, and I'll soak the stains in salt,' Jake snapped.

'I. . . .'

'Look, it won't be the first time I've seen you in

your underwear,' he reminded her sardonically, 'and that wine is going to stain. Come with me.' He reached for her wrist, steel fingers closing round the slender bones as he led her to the stairs and up them, pushing open his bedroom door, and leaving her standing there like a wooden puppet as he opened a cupboard door and removed a shirt. 'Here, take off your skirt and blouse and put this on.'

The dark red stain was already sinking deeper into her clothes, jerking her out of her lethargy. It they weren't soaked in some stain remover now, she'd never get the stain out. Quickly with numb fingers she started to unfasten her blouse, turning her back on Jake, wishing he would go away and leave her alone. Obviously any intimacy between them didn't have the same effect on him as it did on her. As she reached the last button on her blouse she heard his impatient exclamation and turned automatically.

'Give me that,' he instructed, as she started to slide the silk off her arms. She felt acutely vulnerable standing before him in just her silk camisole, her fingers fumbling with the zip of her skirt, which Jake bent to scoop up as it fell to the floor. 'You'd better take that off as well,' he added calmly, glancing at her camisole, 'unless you want it to be permanently stained.' The wine had soaked through her blouse, staining the soft cream silk beneath, and Kate bit her lip angrily as she studied it. The camisole was new and pure silk, and Jake was right, it would stain. But she wasn't wearing anything beneath it, and she felt reluctant to remove it in his presence. He seemed to have read her mind. 'I'll turn my back if that's what's worrying you, although I don't know why I should. I won't be seeing anything I haven't seen—and touched—many times before, will I?'

He was right and she was being childish, but knowing that didn't make it any easier to turn her back to him and wriggle out of the camisole. The shirt he had offered her lay on the bed and she reached for it, tensing as her fingers brushed his arm, her eyes opening wide in the shock of the contact.

'I'll leave these to soak in the bathroom while I get some salt.'

'I really ought to go home, Jake,' Kate protested. She couldn't sit down and discuss their divorce with him, dressed only in silk stockings, a wisp of a suspender belt, a pair of minute briefs and his shirt. She felt too acutely uncomfortable.

'Jake?' She looked over her shoulder just in time to see the door to the en-suite bathroom closing and the sound of water gushing from the taps.

There must have been another door from the bathroom on to the landing, because the next time Kate saw him it was as he walked lithely up the stairs carrying a container of salt, his shirt unfastened at the throat, the sleeves rolled back. Her knees seemed to turn to water, and she had to edge towards the bed, terrified that her legs would collapse under her. Why was he affecting her like this now, when she had never felt a tenth of this avid hunger for the sight and touch of him during their marriage? She wanted desperately to reach out and touch him, to run her fingertips through those crisp hairs darkening his chest and feel his muscles clench beneath her delicate assault. Her eyes lifted to his mouth, her breath caught in her throat as she tried to drag them away from the sensual curve of his lower lip, her tongue unconsciously moistening the dry tension of her own lips as her body pulsed with the need to feel his mouth against her own.

'Kate?' He came towards her and her senses swam with awareness of him; the male scent of his body; the cool tang of the lotion he wore; the movement of bone and sinew beneath his clothes. It was all that she could do not to cry out to him, begging him to touch her. The intensity of her feelings appalled her. She felt as though she had strayed into another world, where she was unfamiliar to herself. The power of her body's hunger for him amazed her. Where had it come from? Had it lain dormant all the time they had been apart? During their marriage she had still been very much a child. Oh, she loved him, but she had also resented and been in awe of him; now she was an adult and she wanted him as a woman wants a man.

'Kate, are you all right?' How could she feel like this and Jake not know about it? she thought dazedly as she felt his hands on her shoulders, his voice rough with concern. 'Kate. . . .'

He stopped as someone opened the front door. 'It must be Mrs Hillary,' Kate whispered, not knowing why she felt this need to keep her voice low. Jake was frowning, but his hands remained on her shoulders, and Kate tensed, her eyes widening in shock as the living room door opened and Rita stepped inside.

'Jake darling, where are you?'

'Up here—what do you want, Rita?'

Kate gasped, trying to pull away, but Jake's fingers tightened on her shoulders and they both heard Rita coming upstairs. 'Jake, please,' Kate begged in an agonised whisper, all too conscious of the fact that she was wearing little other than Jake's shirt, which she hadn't even had time to button, and that Jake himself was practically bare to the waist. As her fingers gripped the edges of her borrowed shirt and tried to tug it together, his hand moved downwards, clamping over hers.

'Don't,' he growled softly against her. 'I like seeing you like that, it's very alluring.'

'But Rita'—Kate protested, unable to believe he could act so coolly, knowing all too well what conclusion Rita would leap to when she saw them, and Jake seemed to be doing nothing at all about it.

'I thought I'd pop round and see you, darling. I've borrowed Mrs Hillary's key. Aren't you pleased to see me?' Rita stepped into the room, her eyes narrowing in disbelief as she saw Kate, to all intents and purposes in Jake's arms. Jake watched her without pity, and Kate felt herself tremble in reaction to the other girl's humiliation.

After what seemed like a lifetime Rita retreated to the door, her eyes glittering ice blue fire. 'Enjoy him,' she flung at Kate as she left, 'because you'll never get to keep him!' They heard her heels clattering down the stairs and then the front door close behind her.

'I think I'll have to have a word with Mrs Hillary about just who she gives my key to,' was all Jake said when the reverberations of the slammed door had finally faded away. Kate realised that he was still holding her, and moved away, freed instantly this time, sitting down on the bed as she tried to gain control of her shaky legs and even shakier thoughts.

'How could you do that?' she whispered at last. 'Jake, how could you humiliate her—and me—like that?'

'She asked for it,' he responded, shrugging aside her words. 'Like any other man who senses a trap is being set for him, I fought back. Rita's set her mind on marriage, and. . . .'

'And to stop her, you let her think you and I are lovers? You realise it will be all round Woolerton by tomorrow? Oh, Jake, how could you do this to me? The Dales aren't London. There's still a certain moral code; a standard that's expected . . .' she began fretfully, silenced when Jake interrupted.

'You could always tell the truth. That you don't go in for one-night stands and that I'm your husband.'

'But we're getting a divorce.' Her breath seemed stifled in her throat, and it hurt to say the words. Again Jake shrugged.

'We could have been trying for a reconciliation. In fact. . . .'

As he bent towards her Kate knew she should move, because his intention was clearly readable in his eyes, but somehow the will to do anything seemed to have deserted her, and her body welcomed the taut strength of his hands gripping her arms with a surge of savage pleasure that was reflected in her eyes.

'Don't fight me, Kate,' Jake murmured. 'You're as hungry for me as I am for you. No, don't say anything,' he told her as his hands slid down her arms to where her fingers were still knotted in his borrowed shirt. Gently he unlaced them, his mouth touching butterfly-light kisses against her eyelids until they closed, and the ensuing darkness abandoned her to a sea of sensation. Without being aware of it she must have moved, closing the distance between them, and she heard Jake's husky sound of satisfaction as her fingers came free of the shirt, his palms smoothing the pale skin of her waist as they slid round her back, shaping her against him. Had she actually known this pleasure before? Kate wondered dizzily, as her arms automatically locked round his neck, the rough abrasion of the dark hair matting his chest, something between pleasure and pain against the sensitive fullness of her breasts, the light kisses with which Jake bemused her powers of thinking, igniting a hunger that held her helpless in its voracity.

'Kate, Kate, I want you so much,' she heard Jake mutter urgently, 'Ever since that night in that damned hut I've been thinking about you like this, hungry for me making those little cries of pleasure that turn my bones to water. Mmm. What is it you want, little Cat?' he asked her as his lips continued to torment her, still withholding the contact she wanted, muscles riding in her throat as she lifted her face blindly to his, too frightened of collapsing at his feet to let go of him and her blood wild for the hard pressure of his mouth against him, murmuring softly seductive questions to match the brief kisses which promised so much and gave so little.

Reason, pride, logic all fled before the devastation of the storm inside her. There came a time when she could endure the teasing no more; when the mere contact of his hard body along the length of hers was not enough and her hands were forced to unwind from his shoulders, her eyes deep, dark pools of sapphire hazed with desire, her hands sliding into the thickness of his hair to shape his skull and stop the languid teasing of his mouth.

'Jake.' His name reached her; blurred and unfamiliar as though her tongue stumbled over it. He bent his head, his tongue investigating the moist corner of her mouth. 'Jake, kiss me. . . .' At any other time the anguished plea would have appalled her, as would his reaction to it.

'I thought I was,' he whispered against her throat, stroking his fingers along its smoothness as she arched automatically beneath the caress. His tongue touched lightly against her ear, and a shudder of pleasure shivered through her.

'No, not like that,' she protested, tugging his hair and trying to reach him.

'No? Like this, then?' Teasing lips delicately explored the outline of hers, moving away the moment she tried to prolong the contact, and then returning to torment her still further, until she gasped.

'No . . . not like that.'

'Then show me.' Kate looked up at him warily, but the dark head wasn't moving, and the grey eyes were watching her steadily. All she had to do was lift her head and. . . . Her tongue touched tentatively along his mouth, her teeth tugging hungrily at the full bottom lip. Tears of frustration weren't far away. He had done this deliberately, damn him, to humiliate her! She started to pull away and his fingers curled round her neck, holding her against him. His mouth was a breath away from hers, when he asked softly, 'Like this, Kate?'

It was everything her starved senses had clamoured for; an intimate welding of flesh and need, a fusion that made her melt into him, conscious of nothing but the heated demand of his mouth as it moved against hers, touching, tasting. As he felt her response he gave a soft groan of pleasure deep in his throat, his hands moving down to her waist and then upwards, easing her gently away from him, as though he shared her reluctance to be deprived of the warm contact with her flesh. The intimate exploration of his mouth was a penetration that left her weak with need, wildly impatient to touch him as intimately as he was touching her. He pulled his mouth away, burying it in the scented warmth of her throat, his fingers tangling in her hair.

'God, the things you do to me,' he groaned. 'Do I have to *tell* you?' he demanded huskily, dark eyebrows rising when she simply stared at him. 'Can't you feel the way my body reacts to you?'

To her, or to any woman? Kate wondered bleakly, suddenly feeling cold. In view of the provocation she had given him it was hardly any wonder that he was aroused. And he was; even if he hadn't told her she would have known it. His hands had slid to her hips, biting into her skin as he eased her against his body, and for one wild moment hers cried out for the feel of him against her without the restriction imposed by their clothes.

'Kate.' He had sensed her withdrawal and tensed slightly.

'Jake, we can't do this,' she reasoned with him, trying to steady her pulse rate. 'I believe it's quite common when people are splitting up for them to feel ... desire for one another, but if we give in to it. ...'

'What are you trying to say? That abstinence is good for the soul? That depriving ourselves of what we both want is going to sweeten our tempers? Or was it all just another game, Kate; a let's-see-how-far-we-can-push-him-this-time ploy? Well, this time, my little Cat, you've pushed me too far,' he growled menacingly, 'and I'm not going to back down—I did too much of that when we were together.'

'Jake, no, you can't mean this,' Kate protested as he swung her off the floor and on to the bed. She tried to scramble off the other side, but his weight imprisoned her, his voice raw with anger as she hit out at him, catching him a glancing blow.

'Hell-cat,' he muttered thickly, 'but you're not going to get away with it this time, Kate. There was plenty of time to stop earlier on.'

She stifled a small scream as his hands wrenched the shirt off her shoulders, using it to trap her arms beneath her denying all her writhing efforts to escape.

'Keep on moving like that and you'd drive a saint out of his mind,' Jake warned hoarsely as she continued to try to escape, and she stilled, suddenly realising that the thrashing struggles of her body had revealed it to him from the waist upwards.

'Kiss me, you begged,' Jake ground out above her. 'Like this, Kate?' And the pressure of his mouth on hers was a cruel punishment that ravished its soft vulnerability, the savage sweep of his hands over her body an invasion that made her shudder in fear.

'Jake, no!' She moaned her protest from swollen lips, turning her head from side to side as she tried to escape, but he wouldn't let her.

His superior strength enabled him to keep her pinned to the bed while he removed the rest of his clothes, and then hers. Kate tensed as she felt his fingers circle her ankle, averting her eyes from the sight of her own body as he kneeled over her, his hand moving upwards along her calf and thigh. Kate shuddered deeply at the wanton desire his touch still had the power to arouse, the circles his too-knowing fingers traced lightly against her skin, circles of fire in the pit of her stomach, an aching, melting sensation spreading through her, drawing her back into a world of sensation. She reached almost blindly for his body, sighing her satisfaction as her hands found the taut muscles of his shoulders, stroking over them and down over his chest, tracing delicate patterns there until she caught his bitten-off exclamation, his hands cupping and moulding her breasts as though unable to deny themselves the sensual contact, his fingers kneading already swollen flesh as she pressed feather-light kisses along his throat and chest, her earlier return to sanity forgotten in the urgency of her senses.

'Kate. . . .' His voice was rough and urgent, shivering across her skin, heightening an awareness which already bordered on the unbearable, the warmth of his mouth as it moved downwards over her skin, gently exploring the upper curves of her breasts and then the perfumed valley between, a torment that tightened her nerves to a sweet agony. 'Kate. . . .' He said her name again, more softly this time as she nuzzled the tanned skin of his throat, feeding on the smell and taste of him. His thumb circled lazily round one breast in ever-decreasing circles, winding the tension inside her until she thought it would explode, the small sound that left her lips when he lowered his head against her a combination of protest and pleasure.

The moon shone almost directly into the room, silvering the broad sweep of his shoulders and arrowing down his back, her own body a fragile sliver of moonlight against the dark possession of the hand cupped round her breast in a gesture so malely possessive that her heart turned over inside her. He had turned her body slightly to one side and lay against her, his head pillowed against her softness, rising and falling with the pressure of her heartbeats, his mouth lazily exploring the firm flesh captured by his hand.

The touch of his mouth, light though it was, was a ravishment of her senses, Kate thought weakly looking down at him, unable to tear her eyes from his face, the absorbed, rapt look she could see on it as he touched and tasted so slowly and carefully that it was she who grew impatient, his name a sob of release on her lips when finally his tongue moved erotically against her throbbing nipple, anticipating in its movement his mouth's possession of her aching flesh, but it never came. Instead Jake released her, lifting away from her to study her flushed and aroused features, her head flung back against the pillows, her throat arched in mute supplication.

'Now we'll stop,' he told her softly. 'Now, when you're aching for me every bit as much as you had me aching for you. No,' he told her bluntly, gripping her hands as she reached for him, 'oh no. It often happens like this with divorcing couples, you told me. The final pathetic conflagration before the fire finally dies, I suppose. Well, lady, you aren't satisfying your lust with me. I won't be used that way.'

'You wanted me,' Kate protested huskily, unable to take in what was happening.

'I've wanted you before and had to ache for you, it taught me some valuable lessons,' he told her bluntly. 'Besides,' he added, 'by tomorrow you'll be thanking me. If we'd taken tonight to its natural conclusions, what would have happened to your divorce?'

He was right, of course, but that didn't make it any easier for her to bear the appalling aching of her body, which overrode even the humiliation of his rejection. She had never dreamed it was possible to feel like this and wondered fleetingly if, in the past, she had caused Jake this anguish. If she had it hadn't been deliberate.

She bit her lip, knowing there had been occasions when she had allowed him to make love to her and then stopped him, but not for this, her mind protested achingly. That was just because she had resented his assumption that he could just make love to her whenever he chose, as though she were merely a possession, incapable of functioning or thinking apart from him. But she had shown him that he was wrong. She had shown him that she was capable of thinking and even challenging his thoughts and his way of life.

'Here, you'd better put this on.' She struggled absently into the shirt Jake had tossed across to her, too engrossed in the line her thoughts were taking to do more than note the sardonic undertone to his voice. Had she deliberately adopted an anti-nuclear stance because of Jake? But that was ridiculous! Every thinking human being knew the dangers of nuclear warfare, and she wasn't the first woman to refuse to have a child because she didn't want to risk her child in any holocaust ... but still the nagging suspicion that somehow she had acted spitefully and childishly couldn't be dismissed. It wasn't pleasant, seeing herself in this light; in fact it was sufficiently disturbing to keep her silent all the way back to the shop, although Jake obviously put a different interpretation on her silence. 'Sulking?' he enquired succinctly, arching a dark eyebrow at her as the BMW slid to a smooth halt. 'It's not nice being aroused to the point where your body clamours for release, only to be told there's none coming, is it, Kate?' He leaned across her to open her door. 'Goodnight, and sweet dreams.'

'You keep on saying that,' she managed chokily, as she unfastened the seat-belt and got out. Her damp clothes had left a cold damp patch against her skin, and she was shivering slightly.

'Umm, but the only way I'm going to know if you're having them is to have you sleeping in my bed.'

It was like a knife slid dexterously beneath the ribs and twisted. Her breath caught and held on the pain, on the memories flooding her mind; on the image of herself in Jake's bed, sleeping in the protection of his arms. 'I'll never sleep with you again,' she thrust at him tightly, wanting to hurt as he'd hurt her, but her strategy was disastrous and rebounded painfully on her when he returned calmly, 'You'll never be asked.'

CHAPTER SIX

'YOU'RE looking peaky, Kate, is something wrong?'

'No, probably just the normal pre-Christmas rush. These trips to London get me down a bit. I'll be okay.' Kate gave Meg a weak smile, hoping that her friend wouldn't probe any further. 'Umm, talking of Christmas, it's high time we did something about getting organised. Matt's asked me to go up to the farm, and you're included too.'

'Thanks, Meg, but Christmas is essentially a family time. I'll be quite happy on my own. I've been invited to several parties. . . .'

'But Kate, what about Christmas Day.' Meg was plainly concerned. 'You can't have Christmas dinner on your own!'

'I'm not going to. I thought I'd ask Sarah to have dinner with me. She misses her family very much and she's all on her own.'

'Oh, Kate, an old woman? I'm not saying she's not good company, but you should be spending Christmas with. . . .'

'With a man?' Kate suggested dryly. 'Oh, Meg, you're a hopeless romantic—you know that, don't you?'

'Kate. . . .' Kate turned, frowning slightly as she saw the worried look on her friend's face. 'Look, I know it's none of my business,' Meg began uneasily, 'but it's all over the village. About you and Jake Harvey, I mean,' she added hastily. 'Now, please don't get upset. After all, I know we're in the nineteen-eighties, but some of the people round here . . . well. . . .'

'What are you trying to say, Meg?' Kate asked evenly. A strange tension was building inside her, a presentiment of what her friend was about to say. 'Well, it's all over the village that you and Jake are lovers and . . . and . . . and you've been running after him, but that he doesn't intend to offer you anything more than an affair.' Meg looked at her unhappily. 'I'm so sorry, Kate, and I can guess who's responsible.'

'Yes, so can I,' Kate agreed in a low voice, remembering Rita's face when she had found her with Jake. 'I suppose that explains the sudden influx of customers we've had lately,' she said in a tightly bitter voice. 'Silly me, I thought they'd come to buy Christmas presents when in reality all they wanted to do was to get a good look at a real live fallen woman. I'm surprised the vicar hasn't been round to lecture me on being a bad influence.'

'Oh, Kate,' Meg protested sympathetically, 'I am sorry, but Woolerton is a small village, and you were seen. . . .'

'In Jake's bedroom, wearing little more than Jake's shirt,' Kate agreed savagely. 'Yes, pretty damning evidence, I suppose, especially when it's been embellished the way Rita will no doubt have embellished it.'

'She's claiming that you stole Jake from her . . . that you gave him what she wouldn't,' Meg admitted. 'Oh, look, I know it isn't like that, that you . . . that if anyone was likely to behave like that it would be her but. . . .'

'Mud clings,' Kate offered for her. 'Oh yes, I know.

No wonder I've been getting so many strange looks recently.'

It left a bitter taste in her mouth to know that people she had thought of as her friends had judged her so quickly and so falsely. And yet could she blame them? All the evidence was against her in so many ways. Illogically, in some way Kate felt as though she deserved their censure. Oh, she knew that legally she and Jake were still married, but the legal tie between them had had nothing at all to do with the way she had felt in his arms; with the physical responses of her body to his masculinity.

She had just finished serving a customer when the phone rang. 'You haven't forgotten that it's the meeting of the Safety Committee tomorrow, have you?' Kevin asked her when she picked it up.

She had! and she felt her stomach sinking nervily as she realised she would be called upon to face Jake again. 'Now don't try backing out on me,' Kevin warned, accurately reading her mind. 'You know what my memory's like, and as for my handwriting——' he gave a groan, 'everything they say about the illegibility of doctors' writing is true—I can't read a word I write!'

Of course she couldn't let Kevin down. The work of the Safety Committee was extremely valuable and surely so close to her heart that she wouldn't jeopardise it, simply because she was too frightened to face Jake.

'I'll pick you up after lunch,' Kevin went on. 'Simon Radlett from Cumberdale is standing in for me. He's as keen as we are to establish some sort of working relationship with the station, since some of the workers live on his patch.'

It was just after two o'clock when Kate heard Kevin's car draw up outside. She was wearing the same suit and blouse she had worn on that fateful night at Jake's. She had wavered over the choice, but it was the most suitable thing she had, and the wine stains had come out, thanks to Jake's prompt action. Besides it was silly not to wear something just because it brought back a few bad memories, she told herself.

'Very nice,' Kevin admired when she opened the door, and turned to say goodbye to Meg, who was looking after the shop. As Kevin opened the car door for her Kate was conscious of the overt stares she was getting from two women on the other side of the road, and two brilliant coins of guilty colour came to life in her otherwise pale cheeks.

'I suppose you've heard all about it?' she asked Kevin tightly as she fastened her seat-belt. 'Rita. . . .'

'Rita did come to me with some story about finding you with Jake, yes,' Kevin agreed mildly, 'but I haven't lived on this earth for thirty odd years, my dear, without coming to realise that things aren't always what they seem. I'm afraid, rather illogically perhaps for a doctor, I tend to trust my own judgments about people Kate, and whether you and Jake are or are not lovers doesn't alter one iota my respect and admiration for you, although I must admit to a feeling of envy—in the former case,' he added with a touch of humour. 'Oh, don't look like that,' he urged her when he saw her face. 'I'm not a complete fool, Kate. I've always known that you and I were too comfortable together to be anything other than friends.'

'It wasn't like Rita thinks,' Kate gulped, dangerously close to tears. She had underestimated Kevin, and that made her feel guilty. He obviously was far more astute than she had realised. 'I didn't suppose for one moment it was,' he agreed. 'Rita has a tendency to see only what she wants to see. She set her sights on Jake, and doesn't want to admit that she took too much for granted. She's made it too obvious locally that she considers him to be her property for her to back down gracefully and so she blames you for the break-up of their relationship. Personally I can only applaud Jake's taste. You do know that he's married?' he asked evenly. 'I only mention it because Rita didn't. She came to me with some stupid story about him turning to you because. . . .'

'I was prepared to go to bed with him and she wasn't—at least not without a marriage licence,' Kate offered wryly, thinking to herself how farcical the situation really was. 'Yes, I know about his marriage,' she assured Kevin. There had been a hint of uncertainty in his eyes when he proffered the information and she guessed that he had been afraid that Jake might have kept her in the dark.

'I only found out because Simon told me. He'd seen it on his medical records when they came to him. Ordinarily I wouldn't have said anything, but having to sit there listening to Rita spout all that ridiculous garbage. . . .'

'I know why you told me, Kevin,' she assured him quietly, 'and I do appreciate it, but there's nothing between Jake and me really. The situation has been blown up out of all proportion by Rita's jealousy.' She didn't say any more, conscious of the fact that although she could explain away how she had come to be in Jake's bedroom clad in his shirt, she had no valid reason for being at his house, alone with him, or at least not one she could offer Kevin, and she had no wish to lie to him.

'Have you made any plans for Christmas?' she asked him, changing the subject.

'I'm on duty at the hospital. It gives the married medics a chance to spend some time with their families,' he explained, adding with a grin, 'Besides, I get to kiss all the pretty nurses. What about you?'

'Nothing really. I've been invited to several parties. Meg is going up to the farm and she asked me to join them, but I feel I don't really want to intrude, not at this stage, so I'm inviting Sarah round to have dinner with me. She's on her own as well.'

'Umm. She came into the surgery the other day, or rather Mrs Simmonds from the Post Office brought her in. She'd gone to collect her pension and while she was there Clara Simmonds noticed that she'd got a very nasty bruise on her arm. She banged into something—very hard, by the looks of it. She's losing weight as well. 'I'm a bit worried about her.'

'She misses her family,' Kate told him, 'she gets very lonely.'

'Er ... well, she'll appreciate spending Christmas Day with you. Are you going to Alan and Mary's on Christmas Eve?'

The Crabtrees' Christmas Eve parties were something of an institution, starting about nine with supper and sherry, going on to embrace Midnight Mass, with a return to their warm, comfortable house for mince pies and coffee before the evening broke up.

'Yes, I'm looking forward to it, Are you?'

'I'm hoping to. I'm not due to start at the hospital until nine on Christmas Day, but you never know. Look, we're nearly there,' he told her as they negotiated a hill and the vast sprawl of the power station lay below them. One of the most modern of its kind, normally it excited a fearful feeling of dread in the pit of Kate's stomach, but today her dislike of the buildings and what they represented was overriden by her unwillingness to face Jake.

Because of the danger of demonstrations and the safety hazards they had to stop at the gates, where Kevin showed his pass.

'That's something that Jake's already tightened up on,' Kevin commented, 'and not before time. During the school holidays, it seems to draw the kids like a magnet and they're forever trying to break in. Jake's suggested taking parties of them round during term time, which sounds a good idea; not only does it satisfy their curiosity, it also helps to give them an understanding of how nuclear power works.' He saw her face and said gently, 'Kate, I know how you feel, but let's face it, nuclear power is here to stay, and we are only talking about a power station here, love, not a missile site, although rumour has it that Jake has worked on missile sites in the past. . . .'

'It's still dangerous, Kevin,' Kate protested. 'Look at the danger of nuclear waste; the mere fact that it can't be destroyed is surely evidence enough of the sort of thing we're tampering with, like children tampering with fire. We think we've got it under control, but really. . . .' She broke off as Kevin turned into the car park and brought the car to a halt. 'Out you get,' he instructed, adding teasingly, 'Got your notepad and pencil?'

Jake had taken over the suite of offices used by the previous director, but whereas before they had always seemed cluttered and casual, now they were almost austere. A smiling receptionist had announced their arrival and they had been shown immediately into Jake's presence. He had been seated behind a plain rosewood desk, unfamiliar in the formality of a dark pinstriped suit, and a toning tie.

'We'll talk in the conference room,' he told them, walking round his desk to join them and indicating another door.

The conference room was a new departure; a part of the office suite Kate vaguely remembered but which had now been transformed with magnolia walls, and a tan tweed carpet, to offset the long oval table with its attendant chairs. Attractive modern prints enlivened the wall, and a discreet cocktail cabinet ran the length of one wall. A little to her surprise Jake didn't go to the head of the table but seated himself in the middle of one length. 'It's more comfortable like this,' he murmured when he saw her surprise. 'I suggest you sit opposite me if you're going to take notes, you'll find it easier to hear that way.'

Responding with a curt smile, Kate started to sit down, colour staining her cheeks as she realised that they were being watched by several of the other members of the committee. The gossip had obviously spread farther afield than Woolerton, but then Rita had many acquaintances. She supposed it was something she ought to have expected, but it was humiliating to be studied so curiously when Jake made the introductions, fine irony in his voice as he used the maiden name to which she had reverted. No doubt every single one of these men bar Jake and Kevin was wondering about their supposed relationship, and the bold manner in which Jake's eyes lingered on her body left Kate in no doubt that he was equally aware of their speculation, but that, unlike her, he did not find anything embarrassing in it.

'I see the suit didn't suffer any permanent damage,' he drawled, finally lifting his eyes from her breasts. Kate could almost feel the swift resurgence of male interest and appraisal, and the glance she gave him was evocatively indignant, although patently of little effect, because he announced to the room at last, 'Kate had the misfortune to spill a glass of red wine all over herself the last time she dined with me. Fortunately I remembered that salt is an excellent remedy against wine stains.'

'I'll have to remember that,' one of the younger members of the Committee murmured, grinning thoughtfully, and under the gentle wave of laughter, Kate forced herself to hold Jake's lazy glance. He had just publicly branded her as his, and had the audacity to look so smoothly pleased with himself that her fingers itched to smack the mockery from his smile. It was left to Kevin to make some remark about getting the meeting started, and although Kate dutifully took notes, it was over half an hour before her smarting thoughts were really on what was being said; part of her still seething with resentment at the way Jake had tried to publicise their relationship.

Eventually though she began to pay more attention. Jake was freely admitting that safety precautions were not as tight as they might be. 'The next time we meet I want to arrange a tour of the station, so that we can all see what progress has been made.'

'What good is that,' Kate interrupted heatedly, 'when we aren't being permitted to see what the situation is now?' She was conscious of being the cynosure of all eyes, and thought she detected surprise in more than one pair of male eyes—probably wondering if her comment was an extension of a lovers' quarrel, she seethed bitterly, as she waited for Jake to reply.

'I do take your point,' he agreed a little to her surprise, his voice bland and smooth, 'but I don't feel I can risk the safety of my staff and outside personnel on a tour at this stage. You will just have to accept that I have toured the station myself, and made firm representations to the departments concerned, telling them that I intend to monitor their reactions.'

'Yes, a couple of Heads of departments have been grumbling about some of your recommendations,' one man interrupted. 'They're saying that it will affect productivity, and the men will grumble about losing bonuses.'

'Then perhaps they'd better ask the men what's more important to them; a little extra in their pay-packets, or their health and that of their families. Productivity will be up again once these safety measures have been brought into operation.'

'The drills you've been making them all do are certainly beginning to take effect,' another man announced. 'We've cut minutes off the routine and the men are beginning to make safety suggestions which we can really use.'

'That's good,' Jake said crisply, 'and it shows that they're beginning to become more safety-conscious.'

'You know that there's been a bit of an anti-nuclear campaign conducted by the local Press?' someone else asked. 'Nothing too heated at the moment, but potentially it could be damaging—a bit of a backlash from all this anti-nuclear fever generated from Greenham Common.'

The condescension of his tone infuriated Kate. Before she stopped to think she said bitterly, 'You seem to think it amusing that women should want to protect themselves and their families from the effects of a nuclear holocaust!'

'Oh, come on, a bunch of hysterical females banding together and kicking up a fuss. . . .'

Kate was about to respond, when Jake said steelily, 'We're not involved in a debate on the pros and cons of nuclear disarmament right now, we're talking about the safety standards in existence at this plant. I for one have a busy schedule ahead of me, and don't intend to waste my time here discussing irrelevant matter.'

Irrevelant matter! Kate's chest heaved. It might be irrelevant as far as he was concerned, but that irrelevant matter had after all been the cause of their break-up. Had it? a tiny inner voice demanded. Was she being entirely truthful with herself? There was a brief knock on the door and the receptionist and another girl came in with cups of coffee. Kate couldn't help noticing the warm smile the pretty brunette gave Jake, and her treacherous heart thudded in almost physical agony. Surely she wasn't jealous?

'I really admire you for what you're doing here, Jake,' Kevin announced when the formal business of the meeting was over and they were all gathered in small groups round the room. 'Your predecessor wasn't half as co-operative. . . .'

'The health and safety of the workforce is as much my concern as the smooth running of the station,' Jake told him. 'I personally do not believe that increased efficiency or extra output can be achieved at the cost of endangering human lives. We're dealing with a very potent force here, and I believe it pays to be extra cautious.'

'How noble,' Kate mocked him tauntingly when Kevin had excused himself to go and talk to the resident nursing Sister about the improvements Jake was making to the medical centre. 'I don't remember you having this humane attitude when you worked at Carlton.'

'Perhaps because you never actually bothered to ask me anything about my work when I was stationed there,' Jake told her explosively. His voice was even, but the tiny muscle flickering in his jaw betrayed him; that and the grim light shining warningly from his eyes. 'If you had done so I could have told you that my work was primarily on the effects of a nuclear explosion; not the prompting of one. Governments aren't, in the main, foolish children, you know, Kate. They're just as aware as you of the potential devastation—possibly more so, but you won't see, will you, that disarming equates with leaving ourselves completely without protection against nuclear aggression.'

'You mean, I'll bomb you if you try to bomb me? I don't agree,' Kate responded heatedly, but somewhere inside her was the niggling suspicion that what he said held a grain of truth. Would a world power that didn't shrink from using violence against its own subjects really be capable of sticking to any disarmament agreement, and if it didn't how long would it be before the temptation to use its own warheads against an undefended nation proved too much? She was allowing the sophistication of Jake's arguments to sway her, she thought weakly, but before she could argue further, another man had come to join them, his expression curious as he said, 'I hope I'm not interrupting anything important?'

'Only World War Three,' Jake offered laconically, turning his attention to the newcomer. 'I just wanted to say how much I admired you for admitting your doubts about your own safety standards,' he offered. 'It was a brave thing to do.'

'Perhaps more foolhardy than brave,' Jake smiled wryly, 'but I don't believe in trying to fudge the truth. In the long run it gains nothing. What I'm concerned with now is for us to work together to make sure that in future the safety standards aren't just met, but could possibly be bettered.'

Kate slipped away while they were still talking. Her head had suddenly started to pound; a result of her altercation with Jake, or was it the confusion of her own thoughts, suddenly nowhere near as clear as they had previously been? She had embraced the cause of disarmament with a fervour that now unnerved her, because it smacked too much of the fanatical. Nothing would convince her that she was wrong about the potential danger of nuclear missiles and she still firmly believed in multilateral disarmament, but she was becoming increasingly doubtful about whether that could be enforced. Her very choice of the word 'enforced' brought its own conclusions, and unknowingly a sigh escaped her half parted lips.

'Tired?' Kevin asked sympathetically, 'We'll be going soon.'

'There's no need for you to take Kate, Kevin,' Jake said smoothly, somehow materialising at their side, his arm resting lightly but oh so possessively against her waist. 'She's coming home with me.'

'Why did you say that?' Kate hissed at him ten

minutes later when the meeting had come to an abrupt and unexpected halt. They were alone in the conference room, but her cheeks still burned from the glances she had received as the others had left. Much as she had wanted to defy Jake, it had been impossible to do so without causing further speculation as to their relationship, and she was bitterly angry about what she saw as a completely irresponsible action on his part.

'You must know what everyone thought,' she added, not waiting for him to respond.

'Must I?' he interrupted lazily. 'Suppose you tell me?'

'They think that we're lovers,' Kate replied recklessly, 'thanks to Rita. And you've only made it worse, can't you see that?'

'Does it matter?' He was busily picking up his papers and carried them through into his own room so that she was obliged to follow him or remain talking to herself.

'Of course it matters—at least to me,' she ground out, almost beside herself with rage. 'Woolerton is my home now... I've built a life here; it's a country community, and....'

'And you've now been branded a scarlet woman.' Jake was actually daring to grin at her. 'Well, you know the remedy, don't you?' His eyebrows rose in mock disbelief when she stared furiously at him. 'Come on, Kate,' he said softly, 'there's no reason why I shouldn't make love with my wife, is there?' He raised her left hand to his lips, kissing her palm slowly, making her go limp with heated desire. 'All you have to do is announce that we're married and *voilà*, the scarlet lady is pure and unsullied once more

... I don't know why you're getting so worked up about this,' he added coolly, 'after all, we've been separated for two years. . . .' He let the sentence trail away into silence, waiting for her response.

'You might have had a constant stream of bedmates through your life since we split up, Jake,' she retorted hotly, 'but I. . . .' Just in time she stopped, realising the unstable ground she was on, but Jake was too quick for her.

'Yes?' he pressed silkily. 'You?' When there was no response he demanded huskily, 'Are you trying to tell me that there's been no one since we. . . .'

He swore suddenly as the phone on his desk buzzed, reaching for the receiver with a savagely controlled gesture that underlined his fury at the interruption. Feeling rather like a prisoner suddenly released from being cross-questioned, Kate turned limply to the window. Why must it always be like this when they met? Why couldn't they meet as adults instead of antagonists? She could hear Jake speaking into the receiver, short clipped sentences, and she shivered, remembering the anticipatory gleam in his eyes when he questioned her. How he would gloat if she knew the truth; that he was the only lover she had ever had—*and the only one she ever wanted!* Stunned by the enormity of the admission, she stood rigidly in front of the window. What *was* she thinking? She started to tremble, unaware that Jake had concluded his call and replaced the receiver until she felt the pressure of his presence at her back. She turned round slowly, compelling tense muscles to move. Just for a second his face reflected her feelings, as though he too felt acutely tired and defeated by their constant arguments; their inability to treat one another as strangers.

'It's getting late, and I'm tired. I'll drive you home.'
She wanted to protest, but he silenced her with a small
imperative movement of his hand.

'No, no more tonight Kate. I'm really not in the
mood. Do you know what I really want right at this
minute?' he demanded huskily, continuing when she
didn't speak. 'I want to go home to a woman who
welcomes instead of rejecting me; who renews me
instead of draining me; who wants to love me, not
fight me.'

'You want to go home to Rita,' Kate suggested,
wondering why her throat should suddenly feel as
though someone had tied a tight band round it.

Jake shook his head emphatically. 'No, Rita's a
taker; as hard as nails and completely without
compassion or true femininity; not the sort of
femininity you're thinking of, Kate, but the sort that
all men dream of and hunger after; a well-spring of
love and compassion that accepts men as they are and
loves them for it, not in spite of it. Oh, for God's sake,
what am I saying?' he muttered wearily. 'You
wouldn't have the faintest idea what I'm talking about,
you never did have.'

It was as though someone had suddenly punched a
giant fist into her heart. For a moment she thought it
had stopped beating, so great was the pain and
distress. Never once in the past had he indicated that
he felt like this, and she felt as though suddenly the
man she thought she knew had revealed a completely
unfamiliar side of himself, a side he had kept
deliberately hidden from her because he hadn't loved
her enough to share it with her. What did she mean,
'enough'? Kate asked herself sardonically. He hadn't
loved her, full stop. Reminding herself of that was the

only way she managed to endure the drive back to Woolerton; that and knowing that the only reason he was giving her a lift was to reinforce the humiliating impression that they were lovers.

When he stopped the car outside the shop she thanked him carefully and got out slowly as though she was afraid she was going to fall in pieces if she moved too abruptly and that was exactly how she felt, fragile and far too vulnerable. And why? Because she still desired a man who didn't love her? Oh no, even she wasn't that much of a fool. It was because she still *loved* a man who didn't love her, and just how much of her defiance and anger against him stemmed not from his job and their conflicting views on it, but from the fact that he had never returned her love, she couldn't even bring herself to think about right now.

CHAPTER SEVEN

'Umm, I love that dress, and it really suits you,' Meg commented when Kate stepped into the living room. It was Christmas Eve and Meg was waiting for Matt to come and collect her. Kate was due at the Christmas Eve party and had elected to drive herself knowing that Kevin, who had offered to call for her, could well be called out. She was wearing the same black Calvin Klein dress she had worn for Kevin's dinner party, a double strand of pearls fastened with a pretty antique knot encircling a sapphire her only jewellery.

The sapphire picked out the deeply intense blue of her eyes, which already looked huge and dark in the pale framework of her face. 'You've been losing weight,' Meg told her almost accusatorily. 'Kate, it's none of my business, but. . . .' She broke off as the doorbell rang, and Matt's entrance put an end to what she had been about to say. When she had waved them both off Kate felt weakly grateful for his opportune arrival. She wasn't in the mood for discussing her feelings—even with Meg. Her eyes went to the fireplace where an ornate card painted on silk bore Lyla's signature. She had also sent a very generous cheque, and ominously, for the first time since their break-up, her correspondence carried no reference to Jake. Did Lyla know that he was here in the Dales?

Gnawing thoughtfully on her bottom lip, Kate slipped on her fox jacket, and checking that she'd got her keys hurried out to her small car. She wasn't going to let herself dwell on how empty the small building seemed; how un-Christmassy, despite the pretty tree she had spent all afternoon decorating. Her fridge was full of festive foods, she had collected the small turkey she would be sharing with Sarah tomorrow, and yet for all her preparations she was conscious of dreading the actual dawning of Christmas morning, dreading the entire Christmas period, in fact. But why? She had already endured two Christmasses without Jake, why should this third one affect her so deeply? Not simply because he was there, surely? No, it wasn't that, she admitted on an inward sigh. It was because she had finally been forced to admit how much she still loved him. Her life wasn't complete without him, and to spend Christmas, of all seasons, apart from him, seemed unbearably poignant.

Her car started first time, much to her relief. It had been giving her trouble recently, and she made a mental note to get it booked in for a service. The day had been cold, but bright, three frosty nights in succession hardening the ground to iron and coating the bare branches of the village trees with silver. Now the moon and stars were obliterated by cloud which must have drifted in during the late afternoon, and as she headed out of the village in the direction of the Crabtrees' Kate realised that it had started to snow. A huge lump rose in her throat; how often as a child had she longed for a white Christmas, for a huge family to spend it with? Her emotions seemed dangerously close to the surface this evening, tears and laughter both not far away, and she wished beyond anything else that Jake wasn't joining the Crabtrees' party.

Several cars already lined the semi-circular drive in

front of the house when she arrived. The snow was beginning to carpet the gravel, and fleck the grass, and the occupants of the car which had pulled up behind her caught up with her halfway to the house, one of them commenting cheerfully, 'Looks like we're in for a white Christmas. Too late to cancel the bikes we've bought our kids in favour of toboggans, though.'

They arrived at the front door together, and Kate was relieved to be swallowed up in the general confusion of greetings. She left her coat in the small downstairs cloakroom and made her way into the Crabtrees' pleasant drawing room. Alan was circulating the room offering sherry, and Kate accepted one, more because it gave her something to do with her hands while she carefully searched the room like a nervous animal wanting to ascertain the whereabouts of its hunter. She spotted him eventually in a corner with Rita and another couple, and unconsciously heaved a faint sigh of relief, quickly overridden by a surge of jealousy so powerful that she wasn't even aware of Kevin's approach until he said anxiously, 'Kate, are you all right, you look quite pale?'

'Fine,' she assured him brittlely.

He didn't look convinced. 'Umm. You're losing weight and you look tired.' He studied her professionally for a few seconds, and on an irrational spurt of anger, Kate demanded curtly, 'So, what's your diagnosis, doctor?'

'Prickly, too!' he commented with a smile. 'It's either overwork,' he teased with another smile, 'or you've fallen in love.' He saw her pale and apologised immediately, concern registering in the warm brown eyes as he tried to make amends. 'Kate, I'm so sorry. That was thoughtless of me, and. . . .'

'True,' Kate supplied, grimacing. She saw Kevin glance from her pale face to Jake's profile as he bent to listen to something Rita was saying to him, her fingers clutching the sleeve of his suit. 'Oh, I know I'm acting like a teenager deep in the throes of her first crush,' she told him wryly. 'I just hope no one else spots it as easily as you did.'

'I shouldn't think so.' His eyes were kind as well as sad. 'Love gives its own power of intuition.' It was his turn to grimace. 'I'm sorry, Kate, forget I said that, will you? It must be Alan's excellent sherry.'

Tears blurred her eyes, and she opened her bag, searching feverishly for a tissue. What on earth was the matter with her tonight?

'Kate?' Kevin saw the telltale moisture and swore softly under his breath. 'Oh, love, I'm so sorry . . . come on, no one will miss us if we disappear on to the terrace for a few minutes.'

Holding her arm, he manoeuvred a way for them through the throng, the french windows opening easily as he turned the handle. Outside, snow just covered the flagged terrace where in summer the Crabtrees often gave alfresco lunch parties. As Kate knew, the view from the terrace was magnificent, but tonight all that could be seen were the outlines of a few bare trees, sprinkled with snow and the edge of the stone parapet round the terrace.

The sounds of the party disappeared behind them as Kevin closed the doors. He glanced doubtfully at one of the wrought iron chairs, frosted with snow. 'I shouldn't have brought you out here, you'll freeze. Here. . . .' He started to remove his jacket, but Kate shook her head.

'No, I'm all right. And thanks for the rescue

operation. I don't know what's the matter with me tonight—one moment I feel like laughing, the next I'm on the verge of tears. I think it must be my hormones, doctor,' she began in a brave attempt at humour, but Kevin shook his head decisively.

'No,' he said softly, 'it's just plain, simple old love. You're in love with Jake, aren't you, Kate?'

She had already admitted it to herself, so what was the point in denying it? 'Yes,' she agreed bleakly.

'I won't offer you the usual platitudes. All I will say is that he's a fool for not. . . .'

'Loving me in return?' Kate's mouth twisted sadly. 'Life would be so easy if we could all love to order, wouldn't it?'

She started to shiver and Kevin said solicitously, 'You're cold, we'd better go back in. Do you feel better now?'

'Much,' she assured him. The cold air at first so invigorating was now chilling her to the bone. Her tears like her heart seemed locked in ice, and cold as she was she dreaded the return to the drawing room and a warmth which would threaten to dissolve that ice causing her to be born again to pain and anguish. 'You go inside, Kevin,' she begged softly. 'I'm okay, I just want a few minutes to myself. I'll be perfectly safe out here.'

He glanced doubtfully at her but didn't argue, and when she heard the french windows close behind him she released a pent-up breath of relief. How unfair the world was! She was hurting because she loved Jake and he didn't love her. She walked towards the balustrade, leaning against the stone, careless of its coldness and the snow melting beneath her hands. As she gazed out into the night the snow continued to fall, white flakes descending slowly to earth, melting when they touched her face. She tasted one with her tongue and felt it melt, absorbed in the wonder of these tiny, fragile pieces of matter which seemed too vulnerable but which when massed together represented a formidable natural force which could and did defy all the technology of man.

She heard the faint click of the french doors as they opened and sighed, guessing that Kevin had returned, his footsteps faintly muffled by the snow. The sudden warmth of his jacket as he placed it round her shoulders showed her how cold she had been and she snuggled into it automatically, tensing like an animal sensing danger, confused by the contradictory information relayed by its senses. The warm man-smell of the jacket draped round her belonged not to Kevin, but to Jake. She moved at the same moment as his arms imprisoned her against the balustrade, the backs of his hands lean and richly tanned against the whiteness of the snow.

'What the hell are you trying to do? Freeze to death?'

'Well, it would be one way of getting rid of me, wouldn't it?' she taunted bitterly. 'You should have left me alone.'

'Ah yes, that always was a favourite refrain of yours.' His voice seemed to come from deep within his chest, and yet it was soft and low, barely reaching her ears, laced with a bitterness which was like jagged teeth sawing at the pain in her heart. 'Leave me alone!'

'Rita will be wondering where you are,' Kate told him tonelessly.

'You'd better go back inside.'

'Perhaps I prefer it out here.' Why was he doing this to her? Tormenting her like this?

'In that case, I'll go back inside. I'm sure you'll enjoy it far more without me.'

'You think so?' He had moved closer towards her and she stepped backwards automatically, stifling a small gasp as the small of her back came into contact with the unyielding stone. Immediately Jake's arms steadied her, one hand sliding beneath his jacket, stroking over the flesh she had just bruised, his other hand spanning the back of her neck, forcing her slowly against him and into contact with the hardness of his chest, the braced muscles of his thighs, his breath warm against her forehead as he murmured something she couldn't catch.

At the first contact with his body she started to tremble violently, a response which had nothing to do with the cold. In fact she was barely aware of the low temperature around them, only the heat which seemed to leap between their bodies, tiny flickers of flame licking through her veins, her legs boneless and weak as Jake held her. She had no means of escape. Behind her was the parapet, and in front of and around her, was Jake, filling her senses just as intensely as the night had done before he arrived.

'I saw you come out with Kevin. What happened? Did you get cold feet at the last minute?'

'We came out here to talk,' Kate lied coldly, shivering at the laughter which began deep in his throat and held a raw edge of violence that tensed her muscles.

'Do you honestly expect me to believe that?' he demanded.

'What are you trying to suggest?' she snapped.

'That we came out here to make love? We aren't teenagers, Jake, desperate for every few seconds we can snatch together.'

'He wants you,' Jake retorted savagely. 'You may not have been lovers yet, Kate, but he wants you. Just like I want you, God damn you,' he swore bitterly. Beneath the protection of his jacket, his hands started to mould her body. She was helpless to prevent him, every ounce of spare energy needed to combat the fierce yearning of her body to throw caution to the winds and drown herself completely in the sweetly tormenting sea of desire enfolding her. His mouth touched hers, lightly, his lips cold, his tongue warm as it moved across her lips in demand and invitation. Her mouth opened instinctively, the feeling of deprivation she suffered when Jake moved almost unbearable.

'Kate.' He muttered her name fiercely as though it was an incantation, his lips no longer cold but burning against her skin as he traced a line of kisses along her throat, his fingers trapping the pulse thudding urgently against her skin and then moving downwards, following the lines of her dress, lingering tormentingly against the swell of her breasts. 'Kate, you want me too, you know you do,' he muttered against her throbbing pulse, the hungry probing of his mouth increasing its uneven beat until she felt she could feel the accelerated surge of the blood through her body, beating up at every pulse point in rhythm with her heart until she felt it would burst through her skin. 'I want you so much I could take you here and now, like a crazed boy,' he told her rawly. 'That's what you do to me.'

His fingers probed the neckline of her dress, seeking and finding the rounded softness of her breast, pushing the soft silk of her dress aside until he had revealed the aroused throbbing aureole of deep pink flesh to his gaze. With eyes which had accustomed themselves to the darkness Kate saw the dark flush of red lying along the line of his cheek bones, his eyes almost black, glittering with a hunger that made her shudder deeply in response, and her fingers automatically slid between the buttons of his dress shirt, stroking the moist, hot flesh beneath. 'Kate, Kate.' Her name was a low moan in his throat as his mouth burned against her skin, the erotic movement of his thumb against her nipple causing her to unfasten the buttons of his shirt and slide her hands inside, stroking him with feverishly hungry caresses, not caring that they were standing almost in full view of the drawing room, or that it was still snowing, her every sense concentrated on the man holding her in his arms, lifting her to a plateau of pleasure where nothing existed but one another.

The deep neckline of her dress afforded Jake an intimacy that brought a fierce sound of satisfaction from his throat, his hands urging her against him, his mouth hotly demanding against hers, coaxing from her a response which left her dizzy and shaken, barely aware of where she was as she tried to get closer to the throbbing arousal she could feel pounding through him. Her head dropped willingly against his arm as his lips explored her throat, his head dark against her breast as he bent lower, merging with the darkness of her dress, his hair dusted with snowflakes. His tongue stroked moistly over one nipple and then the other, cherishing them, leaving both her and himself trembling, and then suddenly losing control, his mouth closed over one erect nipple, his fingers splayed possessively against the rounded flesh.

A fierce shaft of pleasure ran sharply through her body which arched instinctively against him, a delicately responsive shudder he must have felt engulfing her as she felt the faint grate of his teeth against her skin. 'Kate, for God's sake, come back with me tonight. Let me. . . .'

If he hadn't spoken Kate knew she would have followed him mutely to the ends of the earth, but he did speak, breaking the delicate spell that bound them together, and suddenly she was overwhelmingly aware that they were making love like a couple of adolescents betrayed by their emergent senses, and a deep sense of shame overrode the pleasure that had been tingling through her body. She pushed him away, catching him off guard, barely able to look into his face, shivering at the passion she saw there; the half blinded look of need. Her fingers felt frozen as she struggled to straighten her dress.

'All right, Kate, I get the message,' Jake told her in a voice deep with sarcasm. 'Kevin was right to leave you. When he goes to bed tonight it's only his heart that will be aching!'

He fastened his shirt without another word, retrieving his jacket and leaving her almost before she had time to gather her scattered wits.

She realised when she returned to the crowded drawing room seconds later that in all she had only been out on the terrace for about fifteen minutes. At the time it had seemed much longer, but apart from the icy glare she received from Rita no one else seemed to be aware that she had been missing.

The rest of the evening passed in a dull blur. She must have eaten and talked; she remembered going to church, singing carols with the others and then returning with Kevin for the traditional mince pies and another glass of sherry. At one point in the evening she surfaced to find herself talking to a man who was a complete stranger, but who seemed to know her—and her anti-nuclear status. They talked for some time, but later Kate could barely remember what either of them had said.

She left as early as she decently could, trying not to notice that Jake was talking to Rita when she said her goodbyes. The other woman had apparently forgiven him his transgressions, and Kate shivered as she walked out into the thickening snow. Would Rita spend tonight in Jake's arms, in Jake's bed? The pain that followed the thought was a self-imposed agony and one that endured long after she ought to have been asleep, torturing her with images of Jake and Rita together, Rita caressing the male body she knew so well it was no effort to conjure it up out of her memory to further torment her.

Morning brought no lightening of her grim mood. The moment she opened her eyes Kate was aware of the snow. Impossible to spend eight consecutive seasons in the Dales without learning to recognise that peculiar clarity of light; that stillness that invaded the senses alerting them even without the benefit of sight. The snow lay crisp and virgin outside, the sky a clear duck-egg blue. The lights on the Christmas tree offered a poor contrast to the brilliance of the winter sun. Kate moved automatically in the kitchen, preparing the turkey, putting it in the oven, organising the vegetables, setting the table using the red napkins she had bought to add a festive touch to the white linen. A Christmassy table arrangement of gold candles and cones adorned the centre of the table. The gifts she had bought for Sarah lay under the tree along with hers from Meg and Kevin. How pitifully sparse it all was somehow; how different from the Christmases she had always envisaged for herself as as child. She had always imagined at least two children, perhaps three. In these imaginings her husband had always been a vague, shadowy figure, unlike Jake, who dominated every scene he entered. Jake's child. . . .

Her stomach clenched on a fierce surge of pain. She found it inconceivable now that she had ever been stubborn enough to refuse him children. Stubborn . . . she tasted the word cautiously. In the past she had always thought of herself as making a moral decision which she had stood by because her own self-respect demanded it. Why should she now see herself with hindsight as a sulky stubborn child? Jake had wanted children, and she had deprived him of them. Had it been entirely because of her fears of a nuclear war, or had it been partially as a form of punishment when he didn't give in to her urgings to give up his job? How she had resented that job! It kept him away from her when she wanted him, it meant that he came home from work late and often tired. It had taken him away from *her*!

Not liking her train of thought, she gave the table a final check and then set out for Sarah's. She decided to walk, and pulled boots on over her slim-fitting cords, adding an attractive quilted jacket over one of her own jumpers. In lilacs and mauves, it suited her fair colouring. The design was an intricate one— 'snowflakes', appropriately enough, white flakes of snow falling through a deep lilac sky on to the mauve sheep-dotted earth below. It had sold well, and clung softly to her breasts when she moved. Outside the air was as pure and clear as crystal and she breathed it in with pleasure.

It was just under a mile to Sarah's cottage at the end of the village, and by the time she reached it Kate was just beginning to tire. Sarah had obviously been waiting for her, because she opened the door almost immediately.

It had been over a week since she had last seen Sarah, and Kate was dismayed to see how frail and anxious she was looking. She seemed to start nervously at every sound, although she offered Kate a cup of coffee which she accepted, Kate was conscious of her desire to leave the house. Something was wrong, but she knew she would have to tread carefully if she was to find out what. Sarah was intensely proud, as were most of the Dalespeople.

While they drank their coffee Kate admired the cards and gifts which had arrived from Sarah's family in New Zealand. The gifts ranged from the costly down to the homely, the latter obviously bought with well saved pocket money by the more junior members of the family, every one of them sharing a common desire to show Sarah how much she was loved and missed. It could not be because she felt her family was neglecting her that Sarah was so depressed, Kate decided, her eyes misting slightly as she shared her friend's pleasure in her family's love.

After dinner they watched the Queen and then sank into a companionable silence, but all the time Kate was aware that something was missing, and a deep yearning seemed to fill her; a need to share this day of all days with Jake. What was he doing now? Had he been invited to Rita's home? Was he there with her now?

When the evening's feature film had ended, Sarah insisted that it was time she returned home. Kate walked with her, going inside with her friend to check that all was in order before she set out for the walk home.

Even during the short time she had been inside the cottage the temperature had dropped, and Kate shivered, huddling deeper into her jacket, her forehead pleating in a frown as she remembered how skilfully Sarah had avoided her questions. There was something bothering her friend, she was sure of it, but she was no closer to discovering exactly what it was. Could she be having money troubles? For all that there was gossip about her wealth, Kate was worried that the older woman might be too proud to ask for State help if it was needed. She would talk to Kevin about it, she decided; he had the welfare of the villagers very close to his heart.

She was halfway along the village street, trudging along, head down, to avoid the knifing wind that heralded more snow, when she heard the sound of a car behind her. To judge from the soft purring noise of the engine it was only moving slowly and she turned automatically, the blood leaving her face as she recognised Jake's BMW. Where had he been? Rita's? But surely nine o'clcok was early to be going home?

Automatically she increased her walking pace, which was silly because he had obviously seen her and caught her up with no difficulty at all, matching the crawl of the car to her flurried paces.

Winding down the window, he called out sharply, 'Kate, I'm in no mood to play games—get in before you freeze to death!'

It seemed foolish to refuse, and by the look of him

he looked as though he would take any refusal on her part to comply with his command with ill grace.

The interior of the BMW felt deliciously warm after the chill outside. Jake, Kate was surprised to see, looked tired, dark shadows along his jaw. He was dressed casually in a checked shirt and a v-necked sweater, over jeans, hardly the clothes she would have expected him to wear to dine with Rita's parents, who she knew dressed very formally on 'occasions'.

'Why isn't Kevin driving you home?'

The question surprised her so much that for a second her mind went blank, and then she rallied. 'Perhaps because he's working at the hospital,' she replied tartly. 'I've just been walking a friend of mine home. She lives alone at the other end of the village and she isn't all that young. . . . We had Christmas dinner together.' Now why had she told him that? It had sounded so pathetic somehow.

'I had mine in the canteen,' Jake responded shortly. He lifted one hand from the wheel to rub the back of his neck. 'God, I'm tired! I've given Mrs Hillary a few days off, and I decided I might as well go in to the station—it meant that someone else could have the time off. Someone with a family to spend it with,' he grimaced wryly. 'Unappetising though the canteen fare is, at least it was hot. Mrs Hillary promised to leave me something cold.' He glanced out of the car window. 'Hardly appealing in these conditions.'

Almost before she was aware of what she was doing Kate blurted out, 'I could make you something hot.' Her voice faded away, rich colour flooding her face. What on earth would he think? That she had had second thoughts and that this was her way of telling him that she wanted him in the same purely sexual way that he wanted her?

She held her breath in the tension that followed, ready to wince under the sardonic lash of his tongue, but instead all he said was, 'Thanks, Kate, I'd appreciate that. There's something very unappealing about going back to a cold, empty house, especially at this time of year.'

He stopped the car outside her door, and she waited for him to lock up as she opened it. The warmth of the flat reached out to embrace them as they went upstairs, the rich smell of Christmas lunch still hanging appetisingly on the air. 'Umm, that smells good,' Jake commented.

'I could make you some if you like? The turkey will be cold. . . .'

'I'd love it,' Jake assured her. Under the electric light he looked tireder than ever, and Kate snapped it off automatically, plugging in the lights of the tree. In the darkness they came into their own, glittering softly. 'I see you've got a real tree,' Jake remarked softly. 'You always did prefer them.'

'Yes.' She turned away, trying not to remember their first Christmas and the tree he had brought home for her. They had planned to go out together to buy one, but he had to work at the last minute and when she got there the shop had sold out. As a peace offering he had scoured the town for one, and after they had decorated it they had made love. . . .

'You sit down,' she told him. 'I'll go and see about getting you some food. Do you still like roast potatoes?' What a prosaic question, and how much it hurt to think of his tastes changing, his eating habits shaped by another woman during her absence.

'Yes. Kate. . . .' She turned and waited, watching him run his hand tiredly through his hair. 'Do you think I could possibly have a shower?' he asked, disconcerting her. 'It might help revitalise me a little.'

His admission that he was tired worried her. 'Jake, you don't have to eat with me if you'd rather go home,' she told him quietly. 'If you're tired. . . .'

'Home!' His mouth was bitter. 'It's been years since I had a home, Kate, and I do want to eat with you. I'd just like to freshen up a little first, that's all.'

She showed him where the bathroom was, and then went into her bedroom to get some towels. She wasn't aware that he had followed her until she turned and saw him lounging in the doorway, watching her. Heat filled her body as she looked at him, remembering their marriage. 'I think there'll be enough there.' She thrust the towels at him, her voice disturbingly thick and husky, her elbow catching the door which swung towards him. Jake caught it with one hand and stepped into the bedroom to avoid it, his body suddenly tense.

'I see you've kept this.' Kate froze as he fingered the towelling robe hanging up behind the door. It was one that he used to wear when they were married, and she had taken it with her when she left. On her it was huge and far too long, but she found it comforting to be wrapped up inside it. Her 'security blanket', Meg laughingly called it, and Kate flushed as she realised exactly why she had clung so desperately to what was, after all, no more than a piece of cloth. It was the only part of Jake she had allowed herself to bring away with her, and she had held on to it defiantly throughout their separation.

'Er . . . it was cheaper than buying a new one,' she

told him huskily, not daring to look at him. 'Now I'll leave you to shower, and go and see about our meal.'

It was very disturbing to have a man sharing the intimacy of her life again, however briefly, and she was acutely conscious of Jake's presence in her flat as she set about preparing their meal. Her preparations had been finished for over half an hour before she began to wonder how long he intended to spend in her bathroom. The silence of the flat was so dense that she was almost prepared to believe she had imagined him. Concern began to pluck small frowns from her forehead. What was he doing?

The bathroom door was open, the light out. Frowning, Kate walked into her bedroom. Jake was sprawled across the bed, deeply asleep, far too much of his body for comfort, exposed by the robe he had repossessed. His hair was still damp from the shower, a dark blur against her pillow. A huge lump rising in her throat as she studied the relaxed sprawl of his body, she remembered far too easily the intimacy of it entwined in sleep with hers. She ought to wake him, but she didn't have the heart. Surely he wouldn't sleep for very long, and if he did, she could always use Meg's room. If he woke up later and was hungry she could make him an omelette. Almost without her being aware of it a decision had been reached, and her mouth was unknowingly tremulous and tender as she tugged the duvet gently away from his body, tensing only when her fingers inadvertently strayed to his thigh. Jake was beautifully proportioned physically; broad shoulders, narrow waist, lean hips and flat muscular buttocks, his legs long, hard with muscle, compared with hers, rough with the dark hairs that if she closed her eyes she could still remember scraping erotically against her more tender skin. He muttered something in his sleep as she touched him and Kate tensed, waiting for him to wake up, but his lashes did not more than flicker without lifting, the deep, even rhythm of his breathing telling her that he was still asleep.

As she pulled the duvet up round him Kate was assailed by a feeling of indescribable tenderness; almost maternal in its desire to protect and nourish him. In sleep the hard-hewn features softened into rare vulnerability. Her fingers touched his jaw, scraping against the darkness of his beard, the brief touch turning fluidly to a caress which no power on earth could have stopped. It made her ache just to touch him like this, and she withdrew her fingers as though the brief contact with his flesh had burned. How he would mock her if he knew how desperately she wanted to caress the sleeping contours of his body, to waken them to the need flooding through her! Before she weakened completely she bent her head, and brushed her lips softly across his mouth, then she straightened up and walked swiftly out of the room while she still had the strength to do so.

CHAPTER EIGHT

'KATE, are you sure you're all right? You haven't heard a word I've said!'

Kate flashed Kevin an apologetic smile. He had called into the shop on his way home, but he was right when he accused her of having her mind on other things. She had been thinking about Jake, remembering waking on Boxing Day morning to the discovery that some time during the night he had woken and left. A briefly curt note thanking her for taking pity on him was all that was left of his presence. Why had he gone like that? Without a word? The duvet had been left neatly at the end of the bed, the bathrobe folded as though he were in fact a casual stranger and no more. Her tongue touched dry lips as she was invaded again with the sexual tension she experienced each time she thought about him.

'Kate, for the fourth time, have you seen this article yet?' Kevin was brandishing a copy of their local paper. Beneath the banner headlines of the front page she glimpsed her own name, her eyes widening in disbelief as she took the paper from him. 'Like I said, I can't believe you would willingly volunteer such information. Apart from its being a breach of confidence—you remember we all gave Jake our word that we would say nothing about what he had revealed to us, at least until he had a chance to put matters right—the Kate I know would never be so vindictive. An article like this could prejudice the whole future of

the Safety Committee. Kate, are you listening to me?'
he asked patiently, sighing as he realised she probably
hadn't heard a word he had said. She had been too
busy studying the paper he had handed her.

'I never . . . Kevin, I don't understand,' she finished
numbly. 'It says here that I revealed that the safety
standards at the station were well below those
recommended, and. . . .' She glanced at the newsprint
again, as it danced beneath her eyes. '*Well-known anti-
nuclear local businesswoman speaks out*', ran the
headline, and there was a brief description of her and
the shop, all subtly emphasising her anti-nuclear
stance. However, it was the paragraphs which followed
the headlines that astounded her the most. They
revealed in careful detail the deficiencies Jake had
outlined to them at the meeting of the Safety
Committee—deficiencies which had been discussed in
strict confidentiality.

'Harold Barnes who wrote this piece, the editor of the
local rag, was at the Crabtrees' Christmas party,' Kevin
told her gently. 'I saw you talking to him, Kate.'

'Yes, but I never told him any of this,' she protested
feverishly, 'none of it.' Dimly she remembered Harold
Barnes questioning her, but the questions had been
concerning her own views on nuclear disarmament,
and while her responses might have been personally
betraying they had not involved Jake or the power
station.

'No, I'm sure you didn't,' Kevin soothed, 'but the
piece is pretty explosive and does sum up your views,
Kate. Other people. . . .'

'Meaning Jake,' she inserted fiercely. Oh God, of
course Jake would think she had broken her word and
given Harold Barnes the details of their meeting. A

hectic flush stole over her face, her eyes were dark with despair.

'It strikes me that Rita might be responsible,' Kevin offered, further astonishing her. 'She saw Jake going to join you on the terrace,' he added gently, 'and I did see her talking to Harold later in the evening. She's a very dangerous enemy, Kate, and she's judged your weak point well.'

'Yes.' Her voice was husky with strain. 'Jake will never believe I haven't done this purely out of malice, but I've got to try to talk to him. If I don't it just makes me look more guilty. I swear to God, Kevin, I would never do anything like this—never!'

'I know,' he assured her simply. 'But others may not be so. . . .'

'Understanding?' She thought of the other members of the committee, most of whom knew her views on nuclear power. Would they too condemn her as guilty, believing she had given that interview?

'I must telephone the paper,' she said angrily. 'I want them to print a disclaimer. I'll tell them I'll sue if they don't!'

Keven shook his head. 'Barnes will never back down, especially if Rita gave him this information. He won't want to reveal his source, and you've no legal proof that you didn't tell him, just as he has none that you did.'

'And everyone at the party saw me speaking to him,' Kate added despairingly. 'What on earth am I going to do?'

'You ought to go and see Jake,' Kevin suggested gently, confirming her own thoughts.

'Yes—yes, I will,' she told him huskily, 'and thanks for . . . for believing in me, Kevin.'

Long after he had gone the article absorbed her.
Even now with it in black and white in front of her she
couldn't believe it was real; couldn't believe someone
would have the effrontery to twist the truth into this
web of lies and truth which made one indistinguishable
from the other. She was sure Kevin was correct in
saying that Rita had been responsible for the details of
the safety deficiences; her father was a member of the
committee and it wouldn't have been very hard for her
to get hold of the facts. Not only was she destroying
the relationship she doubtless thought existed between
herself and Jake, Kate thought miserably, she was also
probably enjoying the knowledge that she had scored
off against Jake; a subtle revenge for the way he had
treated her when she had discovered them together.
Rita's was the kind of mind that would enjoy that
victory almost as much as she would enjoy destroying
a 'rival'.

When Meg returned from shopping Kate showed
her the article, explaining Kevin's theory. 'It's just the
sort of thing she would do,' Meg agreed, but her
forehead was pleated in a frown and Kate knew
without her saying so that she was worried that people
would believe what they read, and even that it might
affect their business. There was a certain degree of
loyalty to the station in the area, primarily because it
was a major source of jobs, and Kate knew that many
of the villagers did not share her views.

She was trembling when she dressed to go and visit
Jake. She had timed her visit hoping to arrive when he
returned home from work and catch him to put her
case before he saw the article. She couldn't implicate
Rita; for one thing he probably wouldn't believe her,
but she could assure him that Harold Barnes lied when

he intimated that she had been the one to give him the information he had used to such devastating effect in his article.

Her heart sank when she reached the house and discovered that his BMW was nowhere in sight. Even so, she rang the bell, trying to look calm and cool when she was confronted by Mrs Hillary looking wary and disapproving. Her heart sank even further when she was told that no, Jake hadn't arrived back. 'But are you expecting him?' she pressed.

'Aye,' was the uncompromising response, but something of her despair must have communicated itself to the other woman, because she added on a more kindly note, 'He shouldn't be long. Did you want to come in and wait for him? Only it's gone time that I left. I've put him a shepherd's pie in the oven.'

Accepting her invitation, Kate followed Mrs Hillary into the open plan living room, refusing her offer of a cup of coffee and assuring her that she was quite content to wait alone. 'I'll be on my way, then,' Mrs Hillary told her, the disapproval back in her voice. There was a copy of the paper on the coffee table— hardly surprising, as they were delivered freely in the area, and Kate guessed that she had read it and made her own judgments.

Left to her own devices, she read it again, tension clawing painfully in the pit of her stomach as half an hour drifted into an hour and then into two. Where was Jake? She glanced at her watch. It was gone nine. Surely he couldn't be much longer unless ... she gnawed frantically at her bottom lip. How humiliating it would be if he had a date with Rita and arrived back with her, expecting to find an empty house. But she couldn't leave now, with her mission unaccomplished.

If she did, she wouldn't get a wink of sleep. No, she was determined to wait for him. She went into the kitchen and made herself a cup of coffee, turning off the oven and extracting the now desiccated shepherd's pie, comforting herself with the knowledge that Mrs Hillary had expected him back, alone.

Ten o'clock came and went. Across the valley lights started to go out as early rising sheep farmers went to bed. Her nerves stretched to breaking point, Kate paced anxiously over the carpet. When was he coming back? Where was he?

A sherry decanter on the table in front of the fire caught her eye, and she poured herself a glass in a mood of sudden defiance, telling herself that she needed both its warming effect and its borrowed courage. In the event all it did was make her feel sleepy, and she curled up in the fireside chair, telling herself that it wouldn't hurt to close her eyes for a few brief seconds. The seconds turned to minutes, her sleep so deep that she didn't hear the soft purr of the BMW as it came up the drive.

The unlocking of the front door failed to wake her as well, and it wasn't until Jake was bending over her that she came abruptly to full consciousness, her eyes opening wide, the instinctive movement of her body bringing her against him, his mouth a mere breath away as he bent over her.

Her next action was as automatic as it was foolish, a legacy from the days of her marriage when she would often fall asleep downstairs as she waited for him. She raised her face the short distance that separated them, her lips parting involuntarily as they brushed against his, only his smothered gasp of surprise alerting her to the fact that they were no longer living as man and wife; that she no longer had the right to welcome him home with a kiss that invited the merging of their bodies, but even as her hands fluttered up to grasp his shoulders and push herself away, Jake's astonishment gave way to responsive hunger, his mouth moving swiftly over hers, his fingers trapping her face, holding her captive beneath the sensual onslaught of his lips against hers, shaping, moulding, deepening in intensity, until she moaned his name beneath her breath, her hands sliding wantonly round his neck, exploring the shape of his bones beneath the covering of thick hair at his nape, while the heated surge of desire beat up inside her, impelling her to bite hungrily at his bottom lip, nibbling the soft flesh until she felt his groaned response in the renewed urgency of his mouth.

'Kate, for God's sake!' He pulled away from her, the lamplight gleaming on the smooth darkness of his throat as he pulled off his tie and unfastened the top buttons of his shirt as though their presence constricted him. A pulse thudded erotically just below the surface of his skin and she buried her face against the warm flesh exposed by his impatient fingers, lost in the heady possession of her senses by the scent and feel of him, her fingers trembling against the column of his throat, the kiss she pressed against the heavily thudding pulse making him mutter hoarsely beneath his breath, his arms tightening round her, as his throat arched convulsively beneath her stroking tongue inviting the moist exploration of her mouth along the strong line of his shoulder, her fingers impatiently pushing aside his shirt, her teeth biting sensually into the smooth brown flesh, feeling him tense and shudder unable to stem his physical response.

The purpose of her visit was completely forgotten, as her senses took over from her mind, telling her that this was what she really wanted, this heated, almost savage communication which didn't need words; which spoke eloquently of all that she wanted with the merest touch.

Jake was unfastening her blouse, lifting her in his arms as he pushed it aside, his eyes probing the soft flesh barely hidden by the silk bra she was wearing. 'I want you in my bed tonight, Kate,' he told her softly. 'In my arms. . . .'

'I want to be there too, Jake.' She saw the response burning deep in his eyes and was glad she had found the courage to say the words. What did it matter that she loved him and he didn't love her? She had gone hungry for him for too long to deny herself the pleasure his eyes were promising, and as he carried her up the open stairway she knew that tonight she wanted to give herself to him completely, squandering everything she had upon him without thought or caution. Later she could count the cost, but tonight she would belong to him so completely that there would never be another woman who would give him quite as much.

She lay quiescent while he undressed her, not touching him, not speaking, simply watching the unhurried movement of his hands, an answering smile curving her lips as he paused and bent towards her, a soft warmth in his voice that was unfamiliar as he said, 'You're enjoying this, aren't you?' ·

'Yes,' she agreed simply. She *had* enjoyed watching the expressions on his face as he slowly removed her clothes, rather like a small child discovering favourite toys.

'I'm enjoying it too,' he told her huskily. His fingers traced the indentation of her waist, stroking the silky smoothness of her stomach, and then downwards towards the narrow jut of her hip. Kate watched him with an inner hunger which she masked behind an air of indolent languor, watching him touch her body, tensing against the shudder of pleasure coiling through her when his lips brushed against her hip.

'I shouldn't have done that.' His forehead was damp when he leaned it against her skin. 'You go to my head like wine,' he told her softly, 'Just to touch you makes me. . . .' He broke off and watched her as she smiled down at him. 'Now it's your turn to undress me,' he told her, holding her with his eyes so that she couldn't escape and couldn't conceal the responsive shudder of her body, telling him how much she wanted to do just that. 'God, Kate, don't you know what that does to me, knowing the thought of touching me makes you feel like that?'

'I shivered, that's all,' she lied, protestingly, suddenly frightened of the desire she could read in his eyes.

'Mmm. When you shiver like that, I. . . .' His hand had been curved lightly round her breast, and he moved as he spoke, cupping its fullness, his teeth tugging the burgeoning flesh gently, until she arched beneath him, his name interspersed with tiny pleading cries of pleasure, her fingers curling protestingly into the sheets underneath her, not knowing whether to be glad or sorry when he released her swollen flesh. 'Now will you undress me?' he asked her, his voice deep and thick with passion as he turned his head and repeated the sensual assault on her other breast, this time paying no heed to her feverish cries, only releasing her when her nails bit deeply into his shoulders and her body threshed beneath him in a way he knew signified her arousal.

Unlike her, he didn't keep still while she undressed him, his hands and lips moving with increasing urgency over her body as she struggled with recalcitrant buttons and an obstinate belt buckle.

His body was just as she remembered it—darkly tanned, strongly masculine in outline and texture, his skin gleaming like oiled silk, tears stinging briefly in her eyes as she looked at him. He let her look at him, her legs curled to one side as she sat beside him, bending to stroke her fingertips along his skin, as though she couldn't believe he was real. Beneath her touch his muscles clenched and tensed, his body fiercely and unashamedly aroused, and a quiver of something that came close to pain struck through her as she looked at him, but then it was obliterated as he muttered her name with a raw hunger that mirrored her own desire, his head lifting as he pillowed it against her thighs, smoothing the silky skin, and stroking down to her ankles, uncurling her legs from their bent position.

Desire erupted deep inside her, a heady, sexual excitement she could never remember experiencing before, leaping from nerve ending to nerve ending like a bush fire. Long before Jake turned his head and pushed her gently back against the sheets she was aching with desire for him, welcoming his intimate exploration of her body, curling round to stroke her fingers along his spine, lost in a sensual exploration of his body that demanded an intimacy she had never known before. But before her senses had not been starved of him for so long that she wanted to absorb

him into her skin; to feel and know every part of him.
A glorious sense of freedom she had never known
before possessed her, her fingertips teasing light
caresses against his hip, her tongue brushing moistly
across his flat stomach. The sudden tension infiltrating
his muscles stopped her, the heated urgency of his
thick, 'Kate,' shuddering against her skin as his teeth
bit sweetly at her thigh. 'Kate, don't touch me like that
unless you know exactly what you're inviting,' he
muttered against her, his thumb circling the flesh
sensitised by his mouth.

Something primitive and intense boiled up inside
her, a wild sweet yearning centred on the sensations
his mouth against her skin had invoked; a need to
make him share the same desire pulsing through her,
as she ignored his warning, to press her lips
tormentingly against his stomach, her fingers stroking
softly along his thigh.

'Kate!' Jake didn't make any attempt to stop her,
lying tense beneath her tentative caress, until a deep
shudder was wrenched from him, followed by another,
his hoarse gasp of pleasure finding an answering
response deep inside her as he moved, grasping her
hands as he pinned her to the bed, muttering her name
harshly as his lips burned a trail of fierce kisses across
her skin, lingering on the smooth swell of her stomach,
and then lower, tormenting her as she now realised she
had been tormenting him, inciting her to moan and
arch against him restlessly until his hands stilled her
threshing body, stroking lightly along her thighs until
they parted and deep, relentless tremors of need
shuddered through her.

'Kate, Kate, how I've longed to see you like this,
aroused, wanting me, the way I want you.' He bent,

brushing her dry, parted lips with his, stroking them with the moist tip of his tongue, until she melted against him, pleading feverishly with husky, muttered words for the fulfilment his caresses promised but that his body still denied her.

His lips trailed tantalisingly over her skin, the heated, flushed contours of her cheek bones, the delicate curving spirals of her ear, the smooth creaminess of her throat where her pulse thudded out its primitive message, and down, tantalising the firm upper curves of her breasts, the shadowed valley between them, until she felt half crazed with need, her lips pressing hotly urgent kisses against his skin, her hands sliding down his body to grip his hips, the same fine tension infusing her body echoed in his as he muttered something thickly under his breath, her body rejoicing in the slow, deliberate invasion of his as his head bent towards her, his lips touching briefly against hers, tiny, tormenting kisses that ceased only when his body started to move with rhythmic urgency against hers, and the pressure of his mouth finally hardened into the possession she wanted.

She had always enjoyed Jake's lovemaking, even when she resented him, but they had never shared anything like this before; this total giving and taking, for once completely open to each other, both of them revealing the extent of their physical need. Jake wasn't patient or careful as he had been in the past, and the very intensity of his need, overruling as it did the control she knew he was capable of, seemed to ignite a response within her that went far beyond anything she had previously experienced. She was conscious of crying his name as he took them both upwards, pleasure exploding in increasingly urgent waves inside her as she spun, free of gravity in a place where there was only each other, Jake's fierce cries of pleasure blending with her own more muted sounds of love.

She couldn't remember floating back down to earth, but she must have done so, because the next thing she was conscious of was lying satiated and totally relaxed in Jake's arms, breathing in the musky scent of his body, and revelling in the knowledge that it was she who had brought him to that pitch of arousal that had defied self-control.

'I suppose you want a cup of tea now?' He said it drowsily but with good humour, and Kate blushed. It was true that in the past she had always enjoyed a cup of tea after they had made love. 'I'll go and get it,' she offered, but he shook his head, pushing her back against the pillows.

'No,' he growled softly. 'I want you in my bed all night, and if I let you get out now you might never come back. Stay there.'

She closed her eyes, listening drowsily to the sound of him moving about downstairs. She had never known such a feeling of satisfaction. Strange to think it had all come about because. . . . She froze, appalled by the realisation that she had completely forgotten why she had come to see him. There must be something Freudian in her behaviour, she acknowledged shakily, admitting to herself that she had forgotten so easily because she hadn't wanted to remember. Jake had stopped moving and the silence suddenly seemed armed with a distinct sense of hostility. Sliding out of bed, Kate pulled on Jake's discarded shirt and hurried to the banister. Jake was standing with his back to her, looking at the paper. She closed her eyes sickly, and as though alerted to her presence by some sixth sense he turned, his eyes dark with contempt, his face hard.

'You little bitch,' he swore thickly, 'what were you doing? Hoping to get a few more confidences out of me?' He laughed, and the sound was ugly. 'You ought to have remembered that I don't like talking either when I'm making love or afterwards!'

'Jake, it isn't as you think,' she pleaded shakily. 'Please let me explain.'

'Explain? Just how the hell do you think you can do that?' he jeered contemptuously. 'It speaks for itself, Kate. Dear God, and to think I trusted you! I ought to have known better. You're nothing but a crazed fanatic and you don't care who you hurt. I ought to have learned my lesson before; to have realised that the leopard doesn't change its spots. Your damned cause always did matter more to you than me, and nothing's changed!'

'Jake, please, please listen to me. It isn't like you think. I came to see you to explain, Kevin showed me the article this afternoon. I never. . . .'

'Never what? Expected him to publish? Are you trying to tell me that you didn't say this?' He tossed the paper aside angrily. 'I recognise every damned word! I ought to, I've heard them enough. Well, I've had it with you, Kate. I thought you might have grown up, might have come to realise. . . .' He bit out a curse as the phone rang. He picked it up, and his expression changed as he listened. 'Right. I'll be out there just as soon as I can,' he cut in crisply.

'We can't continue this right now,' he told Kate when he had replaced the receiver. 'There's some sort of crisis on at the station. The result of my inefficient safety regulations, no doubt—at least that's what your friend Harold Barnes will want to convince his readers. I suppose it's no use asking you not to run to him with this latest little titbit, is it?' he finished scathingly. 'God, when I think of the harm you've done! Are you so blind that you can't see how I'm trying to. . . .' He broke off, grimacing. 'Oh, God, what's the use? You're so stubbornly blind there's no point in my talking to you. No wonder you put such enthusiasm into your lovemaking! Did he pay you well for that information, Kate? He must have done, to judge by your enthusiastic search for more. Well, at least I gained something from the exchange, I suppose; it's been a long time since my body's known such a quality of satisfaction. You've become an extraordinarily sensual woman in the time we've been apart. I can remember when you would have flinched and drawn back in horror rather than touch me the way you touched me tonight.' He saw the colour rise up under her skin and laughed harshly.

'How long . . . how long will you be gone?' Kate asked tonelessly, fighting hard to retain her self-control. She couldn't leave this house until she had made him believe the truth, but now wasn't the time, when he was so plainly impatient to be on his way. Who could have imagined things could change so quickly, her body was still stupefied by the intensity of their lovemaking, so much so that she was finding it hard to grasp how swiftly events had changed. Five minutes ago they had been lovers. Now they were enemies, at war once again.

'Just so long as it takes,' he drawled coldly. 'Why?'

'No reason.' She wasn't going to tell him she was going to wait for his return. He would probably forbid her to do so, and tell her to leave, but once she left she would never be able to find the courage to return and tell him the truth. If only she hadn't fallen asleep, her ordeal would be behind her now.

But if she hadn't fallen asleep they might not have made love, she reminded herself, and the memory of those moments they had shared was still too precious for her to regret what had caused them.

'I have to leave now.' She had purposely dawdled over dressing, and her fingers trembled nervously against the buttons of her blouse when Jake strode back into the bedroom, dressed in jeans and a sweater. 'I won't hold you up,' Kate told him hesitantly. 'I'll let myself out.'

He glanced at her rather sharply, then nodded. 'Very well.' He didn't offer to wait for her, or give her a lift home, Kate noticed. He probably couldn't bear to spend any more time with her, and who could blame him? He didn't know the true facts, and in his shoes. . . .

She sighed, her ears stretched for the sound of his car. When she heard it moving down the drive, she abandoned the pretence of getting dressed and wandered back to the bed, curling up with her head on his pillow, breathing in the familiar scent of him, squeezing her eyes tightly closed as though by doing so she could prevent the scalding tears from falling. It was a senseless exercise, and there was a certain measure of release to be found in giving way to the misery invading her.

Jake's pillow was damp with her tears before she stopped, suddenly realising that it could be hours before he returned, wondering what Mrs Hillary would think when she discovered she was still here.

What did it matter? Half the village thought they

were lovers already anyway, and once she left. . . . She had to stay, to confront him before she became so cowardly that she couldn't do it. She stretched out, yawning, for the second time in one evening letting herself slide slowly into sleep.

CHAPTER NINE

WHILE she slept Kate dreamed; she dreamed she was back in the early days of their marriage when she had been blissfully happy, believing that Jake loved her as much as she loved him. But that had been before Lyla had inadvertently let slip that Jake had berated her for not watching properly over Kate. From Lyla's confidences she had gained the impression that Jake had married her more out of concern than love, and she had begun to notice that while he seemed content to make love with her he never mentioned his inner feelings or gave any indication that his emotions were as strongly involved as her own. How could they be? she had asked herself, Jake was nine years her senior; and knew far more of life and people than her. She had seen the looks other women gave him, had seen them and been bitterly jealous. In her dream they were together in the house which had been their home before she had become involved in the peace movement and her own personal vendetta against Jake's job.

She woke up suddenly, unrefreshed, drained by the emotions of her dream. In that last final quarrel she had told him that if he really cared for her he would give up his job. How coldly he had looked at her when he countered that if she really loved him nothing else, not even his job, would matter. How childish she had been! She sighed, stretching and glancing at her watch. Nine o'clock. She had slept for several hours, and where was Jake? Still at the station?

She was up and dressed when Mrs Hillary arrived. The housekeeper expressed no surprise on seeing her, merely saying grimly, 'I've heard there's trouble down at the station. Our Mary's lad works there. Came home full of it last night, he did. He's on the night shift and it seems the foreman told them they was all to go home. All apart from half a dozen of the more experienced staff. Some sort of leakage, it is.'

Kate went cold, the blood draining away from her face. She knew all about the dangers of radiation leakage; had seen far too many graphic photographs to dismiss Mrs Hillary's words from her mind. She looked at the telephone, fighting down the urge to pick up the receiver and ring Jake. If there was a leak the last thing he would have time to do would be to speak to her on the phone, but oh God, she wanted to be with him. On impulse she dialled Kevin's number, but his answering service gave her the information that he was out on his calls. Did one of them include the station? Damn it, she swore to herself, she was Jake's wife. She had every right to know what was happening, to be at his side. As she paced the room she found herself praying that he was all right, all their differences forgotten when she was brought face to face with his mortality. And there was the final irony; now of all times she felt a fierce regret that she had not had his child, something of him to cherish and love. . . . 'Oh God!' She wasn't aware that the sobbed words had been uttered until Mrs Hillary patted her awkwardly on the back.

'There, there, miss. I doubt it's as bad as it seems. Two or three of these emergencies they had last year, and all of them turned out to be something and nothing in the end. You just sit yourself down and I'll make us both a nice cup of tea.'

Suddenly grateful for the older woman's company, Kate marvelled that Mrs Hillary had accepted her presence so matter-of-factly. While she was in the kitchen the phone rang, and Kate snatched up the receiver, her terse, 'Yes?' meeting silence.

'Is that Woolerton 8295?' the male voice at the other end asked at length. Numbly agreeing, Kate heard him say, 'I wanted to speak with Jake Harvey. I do have the right number, don't I?' The voice was faintly accented, American, Kate realised, and she pulled herself together long enough to respond shakily, 'I'm afraid Jake isn't here right now.'

'Oh, the time difference, I guess. He already left for the centre, is that it?'

'Yes,' Kate agreed. 'Can I—can I ask him to call you back when he returns?' She wouldn't let herself add mentally, 'if he returns.' She wasn't going to harbour pessimistic thoughts.

'No, it's okay, I'll give him a call another time. Say ...' recognising the hesitation in the sure voice Kate waited, 'I hope I'm not out of line, but are you ... am I speaking with Kate?'

For a moment Kate was too stunned to speak. How did this man know her name? And then realising that her silence must be disconcerting for him she stammered, 'Well, yes, but how did you. . . .'

'Well, that's just fine!' There was a wealth of warmth and pleasure in the transatlantic tones. 'Jake and I were buddies while he was working over here. Got pretty close too. Both of us had been through a bad time personally, and sort of drifted together. I'd

just been through a pretty sour divorce, and Jake told
me . . .' he hesitated, and then continued, 'he told me
that the pair of you had been having problems, that
you wanted him to give up his job. He told me how
you felt about disarmament, and I wasn't surprised
when he decided not to accept the promotion he was
offered over here. I knew he wanted to go home to
you. He told me that he'd hoped to convince you that
by working on the warfare side of nuclear power he
was helping to control its indiscriminate use, but that
you weren't having any, so he'd decided to switch to
the power side. It was quite a blow to us over here. He
was one of our top men—but then I guess I don't need
to tell you how well thought of he is in our field. I
guess he decided that his personal life and you meant
more to him in the end than a successful career. I'm
only glad he was able to talk it through with you.
When he left he wasn't any too sure that you would
see him. He'd been keeping tabs on you, though. That
guy sure loves you one hell of a lot, Kate.'

'Yes.' Was that really *her* voice, raw with pain and
shame?

'Well, I guess I'd better go now, but you might
remind Jake that he promised me I could stand as
godfather for your first child. Say, I haven't said
anything out of place have I?' he pressed uncertainly
when she was silent. 'I mean, you do love the guy?'

'I love him,' Kate confirmed softly, replacing the
receiver. Yes, she loved him, but she loved her own
pride more; too immature to realise that the love that
two people shared between them was such a precious
thing that it deserved to be cherished and protected
against everything else. She was still totally opposed to
nuclear missiles and all that they represented, but over

and above any involvement she might have with the anti-nuclear movement was her love for Jake. With maturity she realised that her motives had not been entirely pure. She had resented Jake's maturity, and her own love for him, and she had punished him for both, cloaking her punishment under the guise of her dislike of his job.

He had actually turned down promotion in America to return to England and take up an inferior job because he loved her! If she hadn't heard it from a third party with her own ears she doubted if she could have believed it. It destroyed all her preconceived ideas of how he felt about her and their marriage. But ... she gnawed worriedly at her bottom lip. Jake himself had said nothing of his reasons for returning to her. Never once had he indicated that he might want her back. Could he have changed his mind? Once he saw her again had he realised perhaps that he didn't love her after all? Confused and anxious for his safety, Kate continued to pace the room. Dared she ring the station?

At last, unable to bear the enforced inactivity any longer, she picked up the phone. When the switchboard answered she asked to be put through to Jake.

When the ringing stopped it wasn't Jake's voice she heard, but his secretary's. 'Oh, Mr Harvey's on his way home,' she told Kate calmly. 'Can I take a message?'

Knowing it would be pointless to question the girl, Kate smiled her thanks and said, 'No.' When she replaced the receiver her hands were trembling. Jake was coming home. Somehow, before she left this house she had to let him know that the newspaper article had nothing to do with her, and then ... if he believed her. . . . She would think about that later, she told herself firmly. First she had to clear herself in Jake's eyes before she started getting crazily hopeful about the future. Things changed; Jake's American friend could have caught him at a bad moment. Jake might have bitterly regretted the confidences they had exchanged; and even his decision to come back to Britain. She could hardly ask him outright if he loved her, she thought ruefully, trying not to remember how they had made love. If Jake did love her surely last night had offered him the ideal time to tell her so. But he had not done. He had said nothing to her of love. Her heart sank, and as she glanced down her eye was caught by the newspaper, and apprehension coiled through her stomach. She couldn't simply launch into an explanation the moment he walked in. He would be tired, unreceptive; probably still mentally involved in whatever had gone wrong at the station. It would be better if she left and then came back later when he was rested.

No sooner had the thought been formulated than Kate heard the now familiar sound of the BMW. Mrs Hillary came in from the kitchen. 'That's himself now,' she pronounced, 'and I was just on my way to the shops. No doubt he'll be wanting some breakfast.' It was plain to Kate that Mrs Hillary was a woman of unshakeable routine, and she offered hesitantly to make whatever breakfast Jake wanted in order that Mrs Hillary need not interrupt it.

'Well, if you're sure you don't mind? Only if I don't go now, Reg Philips won't have a decent piece of meat left in that shop of his.'

Assuring her that she didn't mind in the slightest, Kate tensed expectantly, hearing Jake's key in the lock almost at the same moment as Mrs Hillary opened the back door. She saw him before he was aware of her. His hair was ruffled untidily, lines of weariness cutting harsh grooves from nose to mouth, dark shadows rasping along his jaw as he rubbed his skin unconsciously. He looked tired and gaunt, and Kate's heart went out to him, her body melting with a yearning desire to take him in her arms and smooth away the harsh lines, to see him relax and smile. His head lifted and he saw her, his eyes bleak as he demanded curtly, 'What the hell are you still doing here?'

'I stayed because I wanted to talk to you about the newspaper article, but now obviously isn't the time. Mrs Hillary has gone shopping, I volunteered to make you some breakfast. . . .'

'Very noble of you!' He said it harshly, and Kate could discern not the slightest trace of anything approaching love in his cold features as he turned deliberately away from her.

'Is everything all right? At the station, I mean?' she asked huskily, moistening suddenly dry lips with the tip of her tongue. Her legs had turned to putty, and she felt a cowardly desire to turn and run.

'Yes. It was a false alarm, thank goodness. Sorry if that disappoints you,' he added bitterly. 'I'm afraid you won't get much newspaper mileage out of a radiation leak that wasn't. Is that why you were waiting, Kate? Because you thought you might catch me at a vulnerable moment and that I might say something you could use in your campaign against me? Because that's what it is, isn't it? It isn't just missiles you resent, is it? It's me. No,' he cautioned when she would have interrupted, 'don't say anything.

I've had plenty of time to think this through during the last couple of years. You can deny it all you want,' he said flatly, 'but you weren't just fighting against nuclear warfare, you were fighting against me.'

She longed to deny it, but with new maturity knew that she couldn't. 'I did resent you,' she agreed, 'I admit it, but Jake. . . .' She was about to tell him that she had changed, learned to come to terms with her emotions when an unfamiliar car pulled into the drive. Her first jealous thought that it was Rita died when she saw the man emerging from it.

'Your friend Barnes,' said Jake, contemptuously from her shoulder. 'Nice timing. What did you do? Ring him while I was gone?'

Harold Barnes? What on earth was he doing here? He was the last person Kate wanted to see right now.

Jake was at the door before he rang the bell, opening it to him, his tiredness under control, and a smooth polite mask in its place as he invited him in.

'I hear there's been some trouble at the station,' Harold Barnes began without preamble, although Kate noticed that his eyes had widened fractionally when he saw her.

'A suspected radiation leak,' Jake confirmed coolly. 'Suspected, but fortunately it was nothing more than a malfunction in a piece of equipment.'

'You say that, but, forgive me, how can we be sure it's true?' the editor pressed. 'We already know that there are serious safety defects at the station.'

'There are certain safety defects which I myself brought to the attention of the safety committee,' Jake corrected calmly. 'They are not serious and the station is not, as you have claimed, below the Government safety standards. It is merely that I should like to be able to say that Ebbdale is the safest nuclear power station in the world.'

'A rather philanthropic attitude for a businessman! Surely your prime purpose is to increase the station's efficiency and output?'

'It's certainly one of my aims,' Jake agreed, 'but as I learned during my time in America, there's no reason why safety and profitability shouldn't go hand in hand.'

'Are you saying then that the information we've already printed wasn't correct?'

'I think I'd like to say something here,' Kate interrupted. 'I know I gave you my personal views on nuclear weapons and power when we talked—privately, or so I thought—on Christmas Eve,' she told Harold Barnes, 'but the intimation in your paper that I leaked details of the safety standards at the station to you is something I object to. I never at any time discussed them with you.'

Kate could tell that she had caught him off guard. Perhaps he hadn't expected her to bring the subject up; he had certainly looked rather disconcerted when he walked in and saw her in Jake's living room, but surely Rita had told him about their supposed 'relationship'?

'I want you to print a disclaimer,' she added coolly. 'You see, I do know where you got your information.' She saw him blench slightly, although it was quickly controlled.

'My dear Miss Hargreaves,' he drawled slowly, 'you yourself told me how abhorrent you find the entire concept of nuclear warfare. I accept that you might not remember our conversation it its entirety. Alan is a most generous host. . . .'

He was suggesting that she had had so much to drink that she hadn't known what she was saying to him, and Kate's eyes blazed her anger as she denied his allegation.

'Besides,' he continued thoughtfully, 'it occurs to me that there's more to this story than meets the eye. I confess you were the last person I expected to find here this morning.'

'I came here to ... to. ...'

'To tell me that she wasn't responsible for the leak to your paper,' Jake submitted for her.

'But why should you bother? You've admitted that you're on opposite sides of the fence. Why should you wish to assure Mr Harvey of anything? The article is good publicity for your cause.' He was watching her speculatively, and Kate shivered, not liking the questioning look in his eyes. 'The paper came out yesterday,' he added, waiting.

'And Kate came to see me about it last night,' Jake finished softly. He was standing behind her and she felt his fingers bite deep into her waist as his arm came round her. 'Didn't you, darling?'

'So.' Harold Barnes was openly curious now. 'There's a personal angle to the story as well? That's very interesting!'

He left ten minutes later, and when Jake came back into the living room having shown him to the door, Kate was shaking with reaction and anger. 'How could you do that?' she demanded huskily. 'How could you let him think that. ...'

'That you came here last night and we made love?' Jake offered coolly, plainly not sharing her dislike of putting her thoughts into words. 'Why not, that's what happened isn't it? You came here. ...'

'To explain to you about the article,' Kate broke in angrily. 'I. . . .'

'Had no intention of going to bed with me? I don't recall you protesting any too much, Kate, in fact . . .' he smiled, but the gesture was completely without warmth of feeling, 'last night was the best it's ever been between us. Last night, for once in your life, you were a woman, Kate. Why? What were you hoping to discover from me?'

'Nothing!' She practically screamed the word at him. Why wouldn't he believe her? 'Is it so impossible to accept that I might simply have . . .' *loved you*, she had been going to say, but she held back the betraying admission and submitted instead, 'wanted you?'

For a moment she held her breath as Jake stared at her. 'Perhaps,' he agreed at last. 'I certainly wanted you. I haven't touched a woman in the time we've been apart—I couldn't. That's what you did to me, Kate.'

His admission shivered across her skin, but it wasn't love she read in his eyes as he turned towards her; they were cold and empty, regarding her as they might a stranger, and all her hopes that he might love her died. He didn't. He couldn't and talk so calmly about last night. If anything their lovemaking had simply been a catharsis; and now he was completely free of her. How could it be otherwise when he had virtually given Harold Barnes permission to name them as lovers? He must know what that would do to her standing in the community; to her relationship with her co-anti-nuclear campaigners.

'What's the matter, Kate?' he asked softly. 'Realising what will happen to your credibility when Barnes gets round to publishing today's little revelation? Well, join the club. Have you any idea what it did to me when you persisted in making public your anti-nuclear stance?' he demanded savagely. 'When I applied for the job in the States, it was all down there on my record. And do you know what, Kate? They considered your presence in my life was a weakness; that you might bring pressure to bear on me that would make me crack, perhaps even sabotage my work!'

'But you were soon able to put them right on that score,' Kate challenged back, refusing to yield to the terrible anguish possessing her. 'You told them how little my opinions mattered to you. I was just a stupid female!'

She was going to cry, she knew she was, and she whirled round, fleeing before he had time to realise what she was doing, slamming the front door behind her. Jake made no attempt to follow her, but it wasn't until she was halfway home that she remembered he still hadn't had any breakfast.

Although Meg witnessed her return she was tactful enough not to ask any questions. A trip to London to show the new spring patterns for their jumpers was a welcome break in her week, although Kate found her thoughts returning time and time again to the Dales while she was away. Her sweaters had now established themselves, and she was more than happy with her orders, her business concluded a day earlier than she had anticipated.

On impulse she telephoned her godmother in the South of France, feeling an absurd desire to weep when she heard Lyla's familiar girlish tones. 'Kate darling, how are you?'

When Kate explained that she was in London, Lyla

begged her to stay for another day. 'I'm booked on a flight later this afternoon. You know I always like to spend a few days in London after Christmas before I go to St Moritz.'

Kate knew that her godmother paid an annual visit to a luxury health spa just outside London every year at this time and hid a small grin. Dear Lyla, she was someone who never changed. Promising to meet her at Heathrow, Kate rang down to reception and was lucky enough to be able to extend her stay without any problem.

It was snowing when she went to Heathrow, but it wasn't the pretty, fresh snow of the Dales, and the coldness had a raw, damp quality to it that invaded every bone.

Lyla emerged into the Arrivals hall dressed in lavish sables, her blonde hair immaculately coiffured, her enviable size ten figure hidden beneath the embracing folds of sable, her face unchanged, as unlined as a wax doll's. She kissed Kate enthusiastically, chiding her as they walked towards the exit. 'Kate, you've lost weight,' she reproved.

'I thought a woman could never be too thin,' Kate said dryly. Lyla in a maternal mood was something she wasn't used to.

True to form Lyla had booked a suite at the Dorchester. Kate went there with her, and promised to stay on for dinner. 'Although I haven't anything remotely evening-ish with me,' she warned.

'I can lend you something. You've lost so much weight you'll be able to fit into it.'

'Something' turned out to be a Dior model, and when Kate raised her eyebrows, Lyla said evasively, 'Yes, I know . . . but it was a present. Kate . . . Kate, I'm thinking of getting married again.'

Kate dropped the eyeshadow she had been applying to her lids and turned to stare at her. Although she was used to the procession of men through her godmother's life, it was several years since her last divorce.

'Married?' she echoed.

'Umm,' Lyla nodded briskly. 'You'll like him. He's German, fabulously wealthy, but more important than that, very, very kind. I never told you much about my first husband. . . .' She grimaced faintly. 'I'm not going to burden you with the details now, but it wasn't a happy relationship. He was forty when we married, I was eighteen, and a very young eighteen at that. My parents were quite wealthy and he was on the verge of bankruptcy. At first it wasn't too bad. I had my parents to turn to and your mother, but then my parents died; the money ran out, and Ralph became . . . violent. . . .' Her hand was shaking, and Kate, who could never remember her pretty foolish godmother ever betraying any sign of unhappiness or misery in the past, felt an overwhelming protective rush of love for her.

'It's all in the past now,' Lyla continued bravely, 'but when Ralph died—well, I went a little off the rails.' She pulled a face, laughing at herself and the old-fashioned expression she had used. 'Six months after Ralph died, so did a distant cousin of his, and I inherited everything. For a while I went a little mad; perhaps I even used all those nice young men as a means of punishing Ralph for the past, I don't know, but then I met Jake's father. He was widowed at the time and he wanted to marry me. I agreed—wrongly, because I didn't love him. Jake was about fifteen at the time, and I could tell he resented me.' She paused, and glanced appealingly at Kate. 'Here comes the bit I least want to tell you, darling. I'm afraid I did a very foolish thing. You see, my ... my way of life had rather gone to my head. There'd been so many charming young men that I couldn't see why Jake shouldn't succumb just as easily. I wanted to punish him, you see, for showing his contempt of me, only I'm afraid it didn't work out like that. Jake most emphatically did not want me. In fact at fifteen he was far more assured than many young men of eighteen or twenty. He made me feel so small and cheap, Kate. He despised me utterly because of his father. ...' She sighed. 'Of course I left. What else could I do? It was a considerable shock to run across him again like that when you were with me. ...'

'You intimated that he wanted to protect me from you,' Kate interrupted, sympathising with her god-mother, even while she could understand how Jake must have felt.

'Yes. When he discovered that I was your sole guardian he accused me of corrupting you as I'd tried to do him. Of course by then I was over my wild phase, but arguing with Jake was like arguing with stone, and I'm afraid I still resented him. I let him think that he was right.'

'And that's when he decided to marry me?'

'I used to think so,' Lyla agreed, 'and I'm afraid I might be to blame for your marriage breaking up, because I told you about it—you always were such a sensitive child. I could have cut my tongue out afterwards, but it was too late. Instead I went to Jake, and told him what I'd done. We had a long talk, and came much closer to understanding one another. He told me that he loved you, but that he felt that you were too young for marriage—not in years but in terms of experience. He was torn between wanting you and wanting what was best for you. He always did have a painfully active conscience. When you parted we kept in touch and. . . .'

'You told him where I was living.'

'Yes,' Lyla admitted. 'Did I do wrong?'

'I don't know.' Gradually it all came out and Kate found herself confiding in her godmother, sparing herself nothing, admitting how much her own immaturity had blinded her to reason.

'I still love him, more than ever if that's possible, because I'm not blinded by my own prejudice any more. I recognise now that love between two human beings is more important than anything else, but that it has to be nurtured; that it's possible to love and have differing opinions on outside subjects.'

'Most women have an instinct that leads them to protect, and to denounce war,' Lyla comforted her. 'I'm sure when you explain Jake will understand. The fact that he's given up his research work for a different type of job must mean something.'

'I'd like to think so, but so much has happened recently.' Kate told her about the newspaper article. 'He can't care about me if he's willing for people to believe we're lovers and that I leaked the information in a fit of jealous pique—because that's how it will appear.'

'He's probably already regretting what he said,' Lyla soothed. 'When you go back talk to him. Oh, Kate, I do so much want you to be happy,' she said softly. 'You're like a daughter to me, although perhaps I haven't always shown it conventionally. Do you know, I was actually jealous when Jake married you. I thought he would take you away from me. I knew how much he disapproved of me, and I must confess that when you first split up I was selfishly glad. Go home tomorrow,' she suggested softly, 'don't let pride and misunderstandings come between you any longer. One of you has to make the first move. Why not let him see that you love him enough for it to be you?'

Put like that it all sounded so simple, Kate thought in the morning as she paid her bill and picked up her case. By nightfall she would be back in Woolerton, and her heart started to thud heavily at the thought. Did she have the courage to go up to the house and tell Jake that she loved him? If she didn't she might spend the rest of her life regretting that she hadn't. The worst thing he could do was laugh at her, and surely that would be no harder to bear than her existing pain; than the loneliness of living apart from him.

CHAPTER TEN

THE house was empty when she got back, and a scrawled message from Meg lay by the kettle, telling her that she was spending the night at the farm.

Making herself a cup of coffee, Kate sat down to drink it when she heard the sound of something being pushed through the letterbox. The local paper, she guessed, glancing at her watch. Heart thumping, she went downstairs, refusing to even glance at it until she was back in the kitchen, her fingers curled protectively round her mug. Apprehension quivered through every nerve as she placed the paper down on the formica top and spread it out. The banner headlines leapt up at her, and sickness invaded the pit of her stomach as she read swiftly through the front page article. It was all there, their relationship; the fact that they had spent the night together at Jake's house; Jake's admission that they were lovers; everything but the fact that they were married, and the cruel innuendoes that her earlier 'revelations' had been prompted by jealousy and the fear of Jake ending their relationship sickened her to her very soul. Jake had his revenge and more! How could she face people when every house in the area would have received a free copy of this paper? How could she face Jake?

She wanted to curl up and die; to hide herself away somewhere where no one could find her again. The article cheapened everything she had hoped there could be between them. Only now could she admit how much she had banked on Jake having second thoughts and recalling the statements he had made to Harold Barnes. She had allowed herself to believe the pretty fairy tale Lyla had spun for her, but a fairy-tale was all it had been; Jake did not love her.

She made herself go through the article again, reading every word, each one of them a stab in the heart. It was all there for everyone to read. When she had finished reading she felt soiled and degraded. Who reading it would not believe that she and Jake were lovers and that, worse, she had given Harold Barnes the original story in a fit of feminine jealousy.

She didn't sleep well that night, suffering from the irony underlining the difference between the way she had imagined her return and the actuality of how it had been. She had intended to go straight round to see Jake, but now there was no point. Just by allowing that article to be printed he had shown how little he really cared about her.

She was awake well before dawn, her body drained and exhausted, her mind in overdrive, tormenting her mercilessly. It seemed an effort merely to face the day. Meg wasn't back by the time she opened the shop, and a phone call from her confirmed that she was staying on at the farm for a couple of days longer. 'It's Karen,' she told Kate, referring to Matt's little girl. 'She's started with 'flu and she doesn't want me to leave her, poor pet. I'm glad you're back. I was frightened I might have to leave the shop closed.' They chatted for a few minutes more, but Meg made no reference to the article in the paper. Perhaps she hadn't had time to read it yet, with Karen sick, Kate decided when she eventually hung up.

The shop was surprisingly busy during the

morning, but Kate didn't delude herself that her 'customers' had come to buy. Oh no, they had come to see for themselves what she looked like, this woman who was having an affair with the director of the Power Station while officially maintaining an anti-nuclear stance. Not even that had been left to her, Kate admitted numbly, when a phone call during her lunch break brought the unwelcome news that the local anti-nuclear lobby weren't too pleased with the publicity she had received. 'You must see, Kate,' Geoffrey Cranwell, the local organiser, had complained, 'this sort of notoriety can only bring our organisation into disrepute. Before we know where we are one of the Sunday rags will have picked it up, and you know how they'll make a field day of it.'

Geoffrey had been pleased enough with the original article, Kate thought grimly when he had eventually hung up. She wondered if there was anyone in the whole world whose concern was primarily for her, and not tinged with their own angles. It was then that she thought of Sarah, suddenly feeling a need for the older woman's calm manner and wisdom. She closed the shop early, wishing she hadn't done when she stepped out into the street just in time to see Jake driving by with Rita sitting in the passenger seat of his car. So Rita had won after all. Pain seeped into every pore; she wanted to lie down in the gutter and abandon herself to grief like a child, but pride kept her chin up and her profile averted as she walked through the village in the direction of Sarah's cottage.

Sarah answered the door immediately to her knock, but seemed surprised to see her, almost as though she had been expecting someone else. The old lady had lost more weight, and Kate felt guilty that her worries had kept her away from her friend.

'Sarah, is anything wrong?' she questioned the old lady, when they were both sitting in front of the fire with cups of tea. She had the feeling that Sarah was loath to prolong her visit, but the good manners ingrained in people of her generation prevented her from omitting the courtesy of offering her friend a drink.

'No ... no, I'm fine, but what about you? It seems someone doesn't like you very much,' she said shrewdly, indicating the folded newspaper by the fire.

'No.' Briefly Kate explained her belief that Rita had been the one responsible for leaking the information. 'And of course no power on earth is going to make Harold Barnes admit that. The whole thing has been blown up out of all proportion,' she added bitterly. 'I. ...' she paused as she heard a loud rap on Sarah's front door, silenced not so much by the sudden sound as by the terrified expression on Sarah's face. 'Sarah, what is it?' She went quickly to the old woman's side, feeling her frail body tremble in her arms. The front door was thrust open and a youth Kate vaguely recognised came in. At first she didn't make the connection between Sarah's very evident fear and the young man's swaggering confident manner. She had remembered seeing him at the house before—the nephew of a neighbour hadn't Sarah said? Whoever he was he certainly lacked manners, Kate thought, eyeing him with distaste as he flung himself down into a chair and helped himself to a handful of the dainty homemade biscuits Sarah had put on their tray. These he crammed into his mouth, spilling crumbs haphazardly on to the worn carpet.

'Got yourself some back-up this time, have you?' he jeered, watching Sarah. 'I thought I told you not to tell anyone about this? What do you think she's going to do anyway?' He jerked his head contemptuously in Kate's direction, adding coarsely, 'Even if she is shacking up with His Nibs up the road. . . . come on,' he added, 'don't waste time. Hand it over!'

Kate had barely recovered from her anger at the way he had spoken about her before the truth dawned. A single glance into Sarah's terrified face confirmed her worst fears. This loutish youth was no young neighbour helping out an elderly woman but a cruel parasite, playing on her fear, using his youth and strength as weapons against her helplessness. Kate felt sickened as she saw the fear in Sarah's face and the triumph in his. How could this be happening in a small place like Woolerton where everyone knew everyone else? She had read about old people being mugged and worse in major cities, but in this country area. . . . And was Sarah the only victim of his greed? There were several other elderly people living in the town. . . .

She was on her feet without even thinking about it, her eyes darkening to sapphire as she looked scornfully at him. 'Get out of here,' she told him furiously, 'before I call the police!' She was going to do that anyway, but not before she was able to reassure Sarah a little.

To her utter incredulity, all he did was laugh. He too stood up. He topped her by a couple of inches, and as she glanced down at his rough hands and filthy, broken nails Kate felt the first stirrings of fear. She was being ridiculous, she told herself, letting Sarah's very understandable terror affect her. He was only a boy, barely fifteen. And then she remembered reading about the physical abuse boys of ten and less inflicted upon their victims; their teachers, and her shudder of dread was very real indeed.

'So you're going to call the police, are you?' he mocked tauntingly. 'I wouldn't do that if I was you, Miss High and Mighty. I bet that feller of yours wouldn't fancy you half so much if you was all bruised, would he . . . and then there's that shop of yours. How would you like to come home one day and find all your windows smashed in? Could happen as easily as that.'

As he spoke he picked up a delicate china figure, letting it smash down on to the hearth. Behind her Kate heard Sarah moan. 'I'll give you the money . . . just go away, please! I've got it all ready for you. . . .'

Instantly it all clicked. Kate remembered that today was pension day, he must call every week to collect his 'protection money', but if he thought she. . . .

'Come on, you've got more than that tucked away somewhere,' he snarled when he had snatched the thin wad of notes from Sarah. 'Don't try putting me off any more either, I've heard all about the money your Stan left you. Come on, where is it? Got it hidden under the bed, have you?'

Sarah was crying, shaking with dread, and Kate, for the first time in her life, felt an overwhelming urge to strike another human being. What sort of monster was he, that he could do this to a frail old lady?

'It ain't no use turning on the waterworks,' he warned her. 'I know it's here somewhere. If you don't tell me I'll just have to look for myself, won't I?'

Before Kate could stop him he was flinging the cushions off the small settee, pulling open drawers and tossing their contents into the middle of the room. Realising that the only way she was going to stop him was by getting help, she started to edge towards the door, but he must have read her mind. Just as she was within reach of it he turned, leaping over the tumbled cushions, slamming her against the wood as he closed it, holding her pinned there with the force of his shoulder. She felt her bones crack under the impact; the stifling contact with his body eliciting a primitive fear that raced sickly through her body.

'Not so 'igh and mighty now, are we?' he jeered, watching her with a feral grin. His skin was pale, his eyes a flat pale brown. Everything about him emanated menace. He might only be little more than a boy, but he was dangerous, Kate knew that. Dimly she heard Sarah crying piteously, begging him to go away.

'Not until you tell me where you've stashed your money, old woman,' he told her. 'Or perhaps you need persuading.' A knife had appeared in his hand and Kate stared at the glittering blade, hypnotised by the light dancing on it. 'Come on now, tell me where it is, otherwise your friend gets this. . . .' The knife rested coldly against the base of her throat, the pulse there jumping frantically. With every breath Kate expected it to cut into her. She could hear Sarah protesting that there was no more money, her voice high with terror.

'Can't you see she's telling the truth?' she demanded huskily, terrified that the old lady would have some sort of seizure if the torment continued. 'You've got what you came for, why don't you just go away?'

'And have you running straight round to the police? Oh no!' He shook his head, grinning wolfishly. 'First I've got to convince you that it wouldn't be sensible for you to go against me. How am I going to do that, do you suppose?' His knife moved slowly in a straight line down from her throat, slitting her jumper to reveal her pale skin. Kate shuddered in sick fear which crawled along her spine as she recognised the lust glittering in his eyes as his knife slid between the breasts. 'I ain't never 'ad an older woman before.' He wetted his lips lasciviously, his mouth going slack.

Nausea churned up inside her as Kate tried not to betray her fear. He was talking about rape, but she no longer found the thought of being terrified by a boy of less than fifteen amusing. He meant it—she could tell by the way he was looking at her. 'I'm glad you were here today. That shop of yours must make a pile. Perhaps I'll add you to my round ... make a regular call like every week. Perhaps I won't even make you give me money!'

Weakened by sickness, her head muzzy, Kate tried to marshall her thoughts, not daring to move. His knife had sliced straight through her jumper and the front of her bra where the two cups joined. The thought of those filthy hands pawing her, touching her intimately, made her stomach heave, but she daren't give in to the fear threatening to swamp her. Just as she tensed, someone knocked loudly on the door. The knife was immediately pressed closer to her skin, in explicit warning.

'Keep quiet,' he warned them both in a whisper. 'Don't say a word.' Twisting her neck, Kate could just about see out of the window, and her heart thumped as she recognised Jake's car parked outside. She didn't waste time in reasoning what he was doing there, screaming his name in blind panic as her captor swore violently.

Everything moved so quickly, she barely had time to

register what was happening. The front door must still have been open, because the door at her back was thrust open, dislodging both her and her attacker, the knife grazing against her skin as she fell on the floor. She could hear Sarah crying and Jake's deeper voice, but somehow she couldn't summon the strength to say anything herself. A deep, dark mist seemed to whirl up out of nowhere, and as she felt herself falling she recognised dimly that she was fainting, observing the extraordinariness of the sensations she was experiencing without being able to do a thing about them.

When she came round she was lying on Sarah's settee. Jake was standing in front of the fire, and on the floor in front of him was her attacker, blood streaming from a cut on his lip, his jaw already swelling ominously. As she opened her eyes she saw Jake examine his knuckles, sliding his hand into his pocket. Sarah hurried into the room, looking much recovered. 'The police are here,' she announced, and again Kate was aware of the world sliding hazily away from her as two uniformed men came in and a brisk conversation ensued.

'You realise that because he's under age, there's not much we can do?' one policeman said to Jake while the other bustled the youth away. 'I'll have to get statements from both women.'

'Later,' Kate heard Jake say harshly, his face contorting as he added rawly, 'You do realise that if I hadn't turned up when I did that that under-age thug would have raped my wife, and that he could have killed her?'

'I understand how you feel, sir.' The policeman sounded sympathetic, but Kate was still trying to take in the fact that Jake had referred to her as his wife.

'However,' the policeman's voice became slightly dry, 'I think perhaps the ... er ... measures you used to. ...'

'If it hadn't been for the fact that he is under age, I'd probably have killed him,' Jake interrupted flatly. 'As it is, he can thank his lucky stars that you turned up before I'd done more than give him a bloody nose!'

'And a broken jaw,' the policeman said wryly. 'We'll have to get him patched up before we're accused of more police brutality.'

Jake had hit that boy. Beaten him up because of her? Kate couldn't believe that she was feeling such a primitive surge of gladness. She had never believed in violence, it was a complete anathema to her, and yet. ... When she remembered her own vulnerability, her inability to protect herself or Sarah, she started to shake from head to foot, unwillingly remembering Jake once telling her that nuclear weapons were as much a deterrent as a provocation. Without them they would all be as vulnerable as she had been, open to the attack of any bully with the strength to attack.

The realisation was so enormous, so contradictory to everything she believed in, that Kate's head ached from even trying to think. Was she actually saying that she sanctioned physical force on a personal basis because it had been to protect her; but that her country must unarm itself because she feared the consequences if it did not because they were a target for other powers because of their missile bases? Did she honestly believe that if they did give up their missiles they would be safe from attack? In an ideal world all countries would realise the very real danger of harbouring these weapons, but how could disarmament be enforced on a worldwide basis? Who would do the enforcing? And who would ensure that the enforcers were above corruption?

It was all too muddling to think through now, but she couldn't escape from the knowledge that if Jake hadn't arrived when he did she would have been a victim of that young boy's aggression. . . .

'Kate, I'm going to take you home with me,' Jake announced, coming to lean over her and look down into her pale face. 'Sarah is fine, she's going to spend the night with a friend. You don't have to worry about her. Don't move,' he instructed when she tried to sit up. 'I'll carry you out to the car.'

He did as he had said, putting her in the back seat, a cushion under her head. When he got in the driver's seat Kate murmured huskily, 'That boy . . . he was going to. . . .' Suddenly she couldn't go on. Tears clogged up the back of her throat, pouring wetly down her face, her body shaken by fractured sobs. She thought she heard Jake swear as he depressed the accelerator, certainly the powerful car seemed to surge forward, and it was only minutes before he was pulling up outside his house, opening the rear car door as he bent to pick her up.

His bedroom was already familiar to her, and when he placed her on the bed, Kate felt too weak to move.

'You told that policeman we were married,' she whispered inconsequentially.

'I'm sorry if you object to that.' He sounded terse and anything but sorry. 'No, don't move, Kate,' he instructed as she tried to sit up to tell him that there was nothing she wanted more than to remain married to him. 'I want to see to that cut. I suppose I ought to have taken you to hospital, but it isn't very deep, more of a scratch than anything else, and I didn't want you to be bothered by too many questions.' He saw her shudder and his mouth compressed. 'You realise what a risk you took when you called out to me?'

'I thought you were going to leave,' Kate whispered. 'I was so scared. Anything was preferable than enduring another minute. . . .' She swallowed, turning her head, and then wincing as he bent over her, using a small pair of scissors to complete the destruction of her jumper.

'It's easier doing it this way than taking it off over your head. 'I'll just go and get some water.'

'Jake, I can manage by myself.'

'Oh, for God's sake!' He sounded like a man at the end of his patience. 'Don't be so damned independent! Have you any conception of how I felt when I pushed open that door and saw you behind it?' He swallowed with some effort.

'I can't understand how you got there—how you knew I needed you?' Kate whispered, not caring what she was betraying. His skin looked almost grey, his eyes black with some emotion she couldn't define. 'I saw you driving through the village with Rita. . . .'

'Yes. Kevin had been to see me, after that second article appeared in the paper. He loves you.'

'Yes.' Kate lowered her head. 'But . . . but I don't love him,' she said levelly, 'and we've never been lovers.'

'I know. He told me that too, and that he suspected Rita of making mischief. That was what I was doing with her. I let her think I wanted to see her for . . . other reasons, and then when I got her here, I . . . er . . . persuaded her to tell me the truth. Next week the paper will be printing a disclaimer stating that you did not give them the information about the leak. I'm more sorry than I can say about that, Kate. All I can say in my own defence was that I was half mad with. . . .'

'Fury,' she supplied, trying to smile. 'Yes, I did get that impression—and, Jake . . .' he looked at her from the bathroom door, 'I didn't come here that night to . . . to get more information from you,' she told him huskily.

She closed her eyes as he disappeared into the bathroom without responding to her comment. When he returned she kept her eyes closed, wincing when the warm water touched her skin. He had removed her jumper and bra, but she felt no embarrassment in her nudity. As he had said the scratch wasn't deep but it stung.

'I saw Lyla when I was in London,' she ventured when he uncapped a small tube of antiseptic cream.

'Yes, I know.'

His casul admission stunned her. She lifted her head to stare at him. 'But. . . .'

'She rang me from London. We had quite a long chat.' Carefully he smeared the cream against her skin. His touch was quite clinical, but she was powerless to prevent the pulse at the base of her throat thudding hectically and when he had ceased his ministrations he studied it calmly for several seconds, apparently fascinated by its rapid movements. 'She says you love me. . . .'

Following quickly on the heels of astonishment came bitter dismay that Lyla could have betrayed her. Before she could formulate any kind of reply Jake got up and walked back into the bathroom. She was suddenly acutely conscious of her nakedness, of the rounded invitation of her breasts, her nipples hard and pertly aroused by his touch against her skin. He came back just as she was struggling to sit up and she folded her arms protectively round herself.

'Don't do that.' His fingers unfolded her arms, his voice softly husky. 'I want to look at you.'

'Jake. . . .' She moistened her dry lips with the tip of her tongue, not knowing how to handle the situation. She felt acutely vulnerable, her determination to tell him of her love disappearing.

'I want to look at you because your body can't lie to me, Kate,' he pressed softly. 'Can you imagine what it did to me after what we'd shared the other night, to be faced with that damned newspaper? I thought I was on the verge of persuading you to come back to me.'

'Come back to you?'

'Are you going to repeat everything I say like a parrot?' he mocked. 'Dear God, Kate, you surely don't still believe my arrival here was accidental? I know you've spoken to Art. He phoned me back and congratulated me on patching up my marriage. Said how much he wanted to come over and meet you. And then I had Lyla on the phone demanding to know what I meant by making you unhappy. Have I, Kate?' he whispered huskily, 'have I made you unhappy?'

'Not as unhappy as I made myself,' Kate admitted bravely. 'Oh, Jake!' she gasped in searing pleasure, her next words forgotten as his hands cupped her breasts lazily, his head bending until his mouth found what it wanted, a ripple of contentment spreading through her body when he eventually released her swollen, moist nipple.

'Oh, Jake, what?' he murmured as he inclined his head towards its twin, repeating the tormenting caress until her body was awash with fierce pleasure.

'Oh, Jake, love me,' she whispered back, no longer caring what she was betraying.

'Only if you love me in return,' Jake told her. The laziness was still in his voice, but it was gone from his eyes and his body was as taut as a bowstring as though ready to ward off any rejection.

'I thought you were never going to let me.' She tried to hold her voice steady, but it trembled betrayingly, her admission worth everything it had cost her pride when she heard the sound smothered in Jake's throat and saw the fiercely possessive gleam in his eyes as his gaze slid over her body.

'Oh, honey, my problem is, and always was, stopping myself from begging you to,' he admitted wryly. 'When I married you you were a child, and no one was more conscious of that than me. I tried to ease my conscience by telling myself that. . . .'

'You were rescuing me from a life of sin,' Kate offered, dimpling, her fingers busy on the buttons of his shirt, exposing the powerful muscles of his chest, pressing her palms against the crisp dark hair that grew there.

'Something like that,' Jake agreed. His eyes darkened as her fingers traced the dark arrowing of hair down over his body, the sudden clench of masculine muscles very satisfactory when his hand closed over those fingers, his eyes resting potently on her breasts. 'Do you want me to finish this story, or make love to you?' he ground out at last.

Kate managed to laugh. 'Both,' she responded provocatively. 'Oh, Jake!' Her eyes were nearly as dark as his, as she pressed her lips impetuously to his skin, breathing in its familiar warm smell, her tongue flicking delicately against the pebble-hardness of his nipples.

His whole body tensed, his fingers biting almost painfully into her waist. 'Kate. . . . he made her name both a warning and a plea, 'if you don't stop now. . . .'

'I want you to make love to me, Jake,' she told him huskily. 'We can talk later. When we touch each other we say so much without words. I don't just want to tell you how much I love you, how much I regret the wasted years, I want to show you. I *was* immature when we married. I did confuse my resentment of your domination with my hatred of nuclear weaponry, but today, when that boy. . . .' she shuddered deeply, and forced herself to go on. 'I realised that it would be almost impossible for there to be total disarmament and the dangers that could ensue if there wasn't. It doesn't change what I feel about the threat of a nuclear war, but it does give me a fresh insight into the complexities of the situation. Nothing is so clear-cut that I can take up my old stance again, and anyway, I had already admitted to myself that what I felt for you transcended everything else. That I loved you so much that there wasn't room for my old resentment—and Jake. . . .' He tensed, watching her carefully. 'Jake, I want very much to have our child,' she told him huskily, seeing the fierce pleasure darken his eyes.

'I did some thinking too when we were away,' he told her. 'I wasn't letting you grow up to be an individual. I got so mad when you kept on rejecting me. I couldn't see that I wasn't allowing you to think for yourself. I was damned if I was going to give in to you and give up my job. I told myself you were just like Lyla, acting like a spoiled child, but when we split up I too came to realise that I'd thrown away the most precious thing in my life. I knew I had to come back and somehow find a way to make it work between us. It won't be all roses,' he warned her. 'We're both pretty strong characters. We can't agree on everything.'

'But we can agree on the most important things. Such as the fact that we love one another,' Kate responded softly.

Jake had closed his eyes and he opened them to study her, unzipping her skirt and removing what was left of her clothing. 'I want to feel all of you against me,' he told her huskily. 'The other night. . . .' He closed his eyes and swallowed. 'You were never like that with me before—so open and giving. Touching me as though you wanted the feel of me against your skin as much as I wanted to touch you. Oh, you were always passionate enough—in the end—before, but there was never a time when I didn't feel I had to hold back a little, to restrain myself from taking too much; from burdening you with my need. . . .'

'It's a burden I welcome gladly,' Kate assured him, reaching out to him, and this time his hand didn't come out to stop her when her fingers teased the dark hair disappearing beneath his waistband. She continued to caress him for a few moments in silence until he muttered thickly, 'Kate, if you don't stop teasing me. . . .' His hands came out to capture her breasts, his tongue tracing molten circles against their fullness, making her arch pleadingly against him, her fingers tugging impatiently at his belt.

When they were both naked she paused to study him slowly. He laughed softly, unembarrassed by her scrutiny of his aroused body, but the laughter died when she bent to kiss and caress him, and for a few brief seconds she was allowed to experience the heady pleasure of being totally in control of their lovemaking, of having him respond blindly to her briefest touch, offering himself to her in a way that went deeper than surface love-play. Both of them knew that he was freely making himself vulnerable to her, letting her know the power that was hers; not just to arouse him physically, but an admission of his emotional need of her.

When he had endured a surfeit of her teasing he pulled her gently into his arms, covering her mouth with his, kissing her slowly, and then more deeply, the ascent from play to passion so gradual that it seemed to Kate that it was something so right that nothing could have prevented it.

His lips probed her mouth, gradually asserting his dominance, and her body yielded willingly, inviting the slow possession of his. With something approaching awe she registered the fact that they had never been quite like this before, and Jake echoed her thoughts when he told her hoarsely that he had never possessed her so completely. The rhythmic movements of his body were so sweetly insistent that she lost herself completely in them, wanting to give him everything there was of her to give; wanting them to be one person; wanting the sweet pleasure of feeling himself lose himself completely in her.

It was all that and more, a climactic surge of pleasure that took him with her, their bodies melting together, time suspended as normality gradually reasserted itself.

'You realise you've totally destroyed my credibility as an anti-nuclear campaigner, don't you?' Kate murmured softly, later, still snuggled deeply in Jake's arms, 'and branded me as a loose woman as well!'

'I've got news for you,' Jake told her, kissing the tip of her nose, his hand stroking gently against her breast. 'Next week the *Woolerton Record* has another sensational scoop to publish. The headlines will be "How Love Conquers All, or Nuclear Power Station Director and Wife are back together".'

'You mean you've told. . . .'

'I've told Barnes the truth, or at least enough of it to ensure that his exploitation of our supposed "relationship" dies with next week's issue.' He frowned and Kate saw the hesitation in his eyes. 'You do want to come back to me, don't you, Kate? I didn't do it to force your hand, I promise you, although I must admit when I first arrived I was tempted to let it slip that we were married.'

'You couldn't stop me coming back to you now if you took a job on the moon with a hundred missiles pointing at the earth,' Kate told him grimly. 'I'm not going to pretend that I'm not glad that you've changed your job, but even if you hadn't I'd still feel the same way about you, Jake. I love you more than I fear a nuclear war. If I died tomorrow and we'd had this, my life would have had some purpose. If I live to be a hundred and we're apart, it would simply be a dreary wasteland of time with no meaning; no pleasure, no love. . . .' His mouth silenced her, the stroke of his hands along her body no longer gentle, and she abandoned herself to him totally without regret. It had taken her a long time to recognise what was the truth for her; the important thing in her life, but thank God she had recognised it before it was too late. She had Jake and their love. . . . perhaps it was asking too much that she should expect life to come complete with a guarantee against fear as well.

'Kate, I don't know what you're thinking about,' Jake muttered, his mouth against her throat, 'but. . . .'

'I'm not thinking about anything but you,' she assured him, stroking her fingers through his hair and nuzzling the warm skin of his shoulder, and as he responded to her touch it was true. There was nothing more important than him. Not now—not ever.

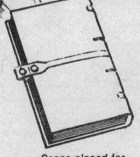

Take 4 these best-selling novels FREE

Harlequin Presents...

ANNE MATHER
born out of love

VIOLET WINSPEAR
time of the temptress

CHARLOTTE LAMB
man's world

SALLY WENTWORTH
say hello to yesterday

Take these 4 best-selling novels FREE

Yes! Four sophisticated, contemporary love stories by four world-famous authors of romance FREE, as your introduction to the Harlequin Presents subscription plan. Thrill to **Anne Mather**'s passionate story BORN OUT OF LOVE, set in the Caribbean.... Travel to darkest Africa in **Violet Winspear**'s TIME OF THE TEMPTRESS....Let **Charlotte Lamb** take you to the fascinating world of London's Fleet Street in MAN'S WORLD .... Discover beautiful Greece in **Sally Wentworth**'s moving romance SAY HELLO TO YESTERDAY.

Harlequin Presents...

The very finest in romance fiction

Join the millions of avid Harlequin readers all over the world who delight in the magic of a really exciting novel. EIGHT great NEW titles published EACH MONTH! Each month you will get to know exciting, interesting, true-to-life people .... You'll be swept to distant lands you've dreamed of visiting .... Intrigue, adventure, romance, and the destiny of many lives will thrill you through each Harlequin Presents novel.

Get all the latest books before they're sold out!
As a Harlequin subscriber you actually receive your personal copies of the latest Presents novels immediately after they come off the press, so you're sure of getting all 8 each month.

Cancel your subscription whenever you wish!
You don't have to buy any minimum number of books. Whenever you decide to stop your subscription just let us know and we'll cancel all further shipments.